A Merry Vested Wedding

NEW YORK TIMES AND *USA TODAY* BESTSELLING AUTHOR

MELANIE MORELAND

Dear Reader,

Thank you for selecting A Merry Vested Wedding to read. Be sure to sign up for my newsletter for up to date information on new releases, exclusive content and sales.

Before you sign up, add melanie@melaniemoreland.com to your contacts to make sure the email comes right to your inbox!
Always fun - never spam!

My books are available in both paperback and audiobook! I also have personalized signed paperbacks available at my website.

The Perfect Recipe For **LOVE**
xoxo,
Melanie

ISBN Ebook 978-1-988610-45-0
Paperback 978-1-988610-44-3

Edited by
Lisa Hollett—Silently Correcting Your Grammar
Cover design by Karen Hulseman, Feed Your Dreams Designs
Photo Adobe Stock
Cover content is for illustrative purposes only and any person depicted on the cover is a model.

DEDICATION

Because you asked—

This is for you.

My readers.

Thank you.

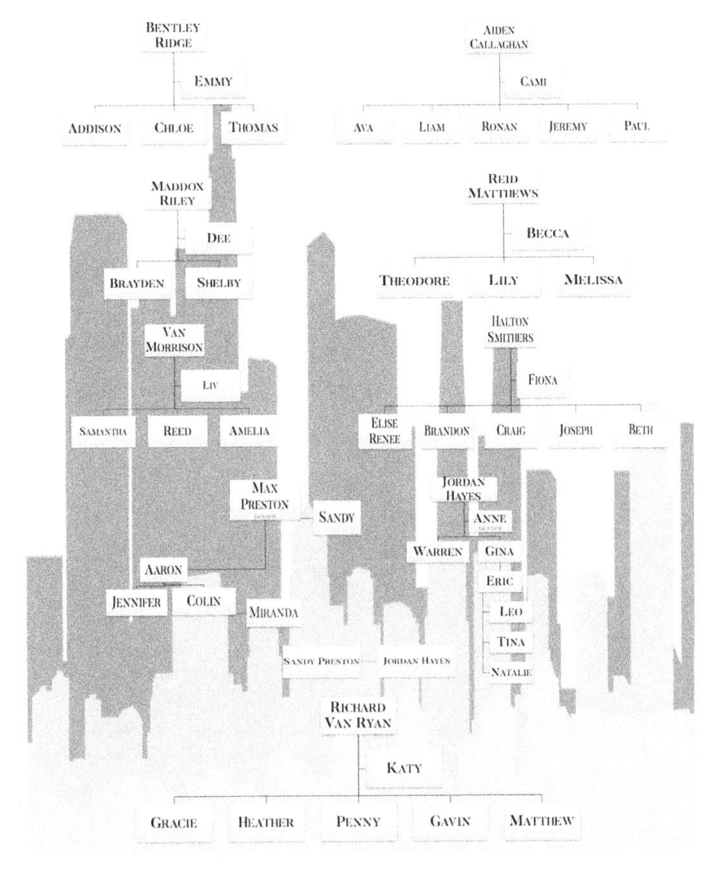

FAMILY TREE

The Contract · VESTED INTEREST

NEW YORK TIMES AND USA TODAY BESTSELLING AUTHOR

MELANIE MORELAND

A BRIEF PEEK AT THE PAST

(Extended epilogue from Sandy, Book 7 of the Vested Interest Series.)

BRAYDEN

The hardwood floors creaked under my feet as I made my way toward the boardroom at BAM. I stopped by the main desk, smiling at Lynn.

"How's it going?"

She smiled in return, handing me a stack of files. "Good. How was the workout?"

I groaned. "Uncle Aiden was in fine form. I swear he's in better shape in his fifties than any of us are in our twenties."

"Speak for yourself." I was hip checked by a lanky brunette as she went by. "I can run circles around you, Brayden Riley."

I chuckled. The ball of fire known as Ava to us

all could bring any of us—her triplet brothers included—to their knees. Aiden, her father, made sure she was as tough as her brothers, if not tougher, physically. She was feisty, strong, and one of the best people I knew. I adored her.

I rolled my shoulders, and Lynn grinned, handing me some Tylenol and a bottle of water. "You're gonna need this."

"Yeah, my body took a beating."

"So will your head this afternoon. The agenda's been added to."

I swallowed the pills. "Oh god. She didn't. Another 'vision'?"

Lynn smirked. "Like father, like daughter. They're both on a roll."

"God help me."

"Go defend your budgets."

I laughed and gathered up the files, heading to the conference room.

At the end of the table, the Callaghan triplets—Ronan, Paul, and Jeremy—were poring over a set of blueprints. Large cups of coffee were in their massive paws. An empty plate scattered with the crumbs of what I assumed were Danishes sat on the large wooden table. They looked up as I walked in, their faces breaking into large grins. They looked like Aiden, except none of them had his different-colored eyes. They were tall, muscular, with dark curly hair and their mother's green eyes. That seemed to be the only thing they had inherited from

Cami. They were big, loud, with boisterous voices and booming laughs.

And all brilliant in architecture and design. A huge asset to the company. If they weren't, they wouldn't be here. Family or not.

A figure rushed past, and the scent of coffee hit me. I grinned at the woman who settled into the chair beside mine, her laptop open, her hands already busy as she waited for the meeting to start.

"Heather VanRyan, is that any way to say hello?"

She glanced up, a small frown on her face. I tried not to laugh at the smudges of color on her cheeks, no doubt from the many felt pens she was always using.

"Hey, Bray." She looked back to her laptop. "I had an idea for a mural in the lobby of the new condo tower. Gotta get it out."

I flicked her hair. "Wasn't your hair hot pink on the weekend?"

She rolled her eyes. "I was told cornflower blue suited my eyes."

Reed Morrison peered over the edge of the two laptops in front of him. "It does. Totally hot, babe."

"Not at the office, Reed. Keep it in your pants."

He chuckled, going back to his screen.

"Not what you said last night."

I tried not to laugh at the two of them. Heather and Reed loved to spar. It was their thing. It drove Gracie VanRyan, Heather's sister, crazy. She was the quiet one, suited to her chosen profession of the law. Unflappable and intelligent, she looked like her mother, with dark hair and blue eyes, while Heather had inherited her father's hazel eyes, the color shifting according to her mood.

Gracie attended the University of Toronto, finishing her degree in corporate law. She planned to come to work at ABC full time once she had completed her internship. Richard often bemoaned that both his eldest daughters were here in Toronto and not in BC, but everyone knew he was pleased for them to be working with us.

Their parents, especially Richard, visited often to check on "his girls" and spend time with my dad. The two of them were the best of friends.

I grabbed a cinnamon bun and bit into it, then poured some black coffee from the carafe, sipping with appreciation. I settled into my seat, wondering what the latest addition would be to the lineup.

I took my laptop from my bag, purposely dropping the empty satchel on the floor beside me.

The distinct sound of stilettos approaching made me smile. The steps were measured, a steady rhythm to the sharp snaps of the heels against wood. The firm steps belonged to someone larger-than-life, whose presence commanded respect.

The person who entered the room did command respect, but not for her tall stature. The golden-haired woman was tiny, her bright hair gleaming in the light. Intense blue eyes swept through the room, in control. She radiated poise. Power. The stern expression on her face suggested an unbending will and lack of humor. She appeared rigid. Unfeeling.

Looks could be deceiving.

A large travel mug landed on the table beside me. An amused voice, low and husky, spoke close to my ear.

"You don't have enough room? You have to use the floor space, too?"

I didn't look up. "It fell off the chair."

Addison Ridge bent down, snagged the handles, and dropped my bag into the empty chair. "You could have picked it up off the floor."

My lips quirked. We had done this many times. How her parents met was one of her favorite stories, and I relived it with her often. "Did you stumble? Are you hurt?"

"No."

"Then stop being such an ass." I winked. "Say hello, Addi."

She blinked at me, leaning close. I could smell her perfume, feel her heat. No one else paid attention to us. They never did. "You can't call me an ass," she murmured, her eyes dancing.

"I think I just did."

"You can't call me an ass when we're about to commence a business meeting."

"But once I get you alone, can I touch yours?" I whispered.

She shook her head, a wide smile gracing her face. It transformed her features, softening them. It was a look few people ever saw, and I was thrilled to be the one who saw it the most. My Addi—my little elf. The love of my life.

"Can the two of you behave?" Ronan groaned. "This is a meeting after all."

I pushed the plate of buns his way. "Shut up and stuff your face."

Addi rolled her eyes. "Enough, boys." She turned to me. "Behave, Brayden."

"Your wish, my command," I deadpanned, then smiled as Addi ran her fingers down my cheek, her engagement ring catching the light. My ring. My girl.

I had loved her from the time I could walk, always gravitating to her. We were always together, although she had resisted once we grew up, insisting we were almost family and it seemed improper.

I was heartbroken, my feelings real and permanent. Finally, Nan sat her down and had a long heart-to-heart with her. Whatever wisdom she imparted helped, and Addi came to me shortly after, admitting her feelings.

We'd been together ever since.

With a grin, I leaned in with the whisper of a kiss. "You have the floor, Madam President."

I was so damn proud of her. A natural leader, she was in control and all business during the day. When Uncle Bentley decided to add another arm to

BAM, Addi was the right choice to run it. We jokingly called it ABC—Addi, Brayden, and the Callaghans. It went well with BAM, and our older, business-savvy fathers loved the idea. So, it became real. ABC Corp.—a division of BAM.

We concentrated on outlying areas. Finding new acquisitions and developing them as a new revenue stream, running the businesses we put into place in some areas. We all had our jobs. Addi discovered, the boys designed, Ava and Heather added the finishing touches, and I handled the budgets. We had business teams for the day-to-day running of the companies we added. It was lucrative and challenging, and we all loved it. Not all the BAM second generation were part of the company, but our parents supported us no matter what option we chose.

Addi cleared her throat as she took in the group gathered around the table, waiting for her to speak. With our fathers' guidance, we continued to make our mark on the landscape of various Ontario cities, always expanding and growing, and Addi was a huge part of that growth.

"Please note the new item on the agenda. I discovered a property while on a detour heading to Port Albany this weekend. An undiscovered, undeveloped piece of property, possibly due to its odd shape and the fact that it is off the beaten track."

Excitement saturated her voice. "I had a vision…"

PART I

PRESENT DAY

CHAPTER 1

BRAYDEN

The morning of December 22, I stood in the kitchen, staring out the window as the sun began to rise. Slowly, its rays lightened the sky, scattering over the beach, glinting on the frost-covered rocks.

Winter in Port Albany was magical. The water in the inlet usually froze, while the open waters farther beyond our tiny cove remained alive and frothy. The sand mingled with snow and ice, creating sculptures and divots everywhere. The trees hung lower with ice, and the ground was often covered with snow.

I loved it here. It was my favorite place on earth. A smile stretched across my face. My favorite place on earth, my favorite time of year, combining into my favorite day of my life.

My wedding day.

Today, I would marry my Addison. My little elf.

Here in this place created by my uncle Bentley—soon to be my father-in-law.

His vision of a special place, a place where family could gather and be together—to de-stress and find your center—had grown and changed over the years. As a child, I could recall the six houses, all clustered—a small community, as it were. All of us kids running around, parents always close. Sandy and Jordan were never far. Adopted uncles, aunts, cousins—there was always someone to play with, hang around with, enjoy life.

The property hummed, especially on weekends. When they added the building we named the Hub, it became the focal point for all our celebrations.

Then our families grew. And my father and his partners knew exactly how to accommodate. They bought as much land as they could surrounding the original six houses. Created an entire village. "The BAM Compound," Uncle Aiden referred to it as.

Twenty houses dotted the area. Some small weekend cottages, some larger live-in-all-the-time dwellings. You never knew who would be there, but there was always an abundance of people.

I lived here year-round. I had loved this place as a child when we would come out on weekends. Unlike my urban-dwelling parents, I yearned for the wide-open spaces of Port Albany. The sound of the waves, the endless scope of the water stretching out in front of me. Often, I begged my parents to let me stay when it was time to head back to the city. Uncle Aiden understood my love of the place and would urge my dad to let me remain behind. I could run and move here. The city always felt more constrictive.

And besides, often when I stayed behind, my best friend was here. My Addison. There was no one I liked to spend time with more than her.

She had always been in my life. I couldn't recall a single memory from my childhood without her in it. Every happy moment, she was there. We attended the same schools, went to the same dances, hung out with the same friends. We celebrated the good moments and bolstered each other during the sad ones. We were always friends.

Until, one day, it changed.

I was sixteen, and it was the start of summer vacation, which meant I would spend most of the summer on the beach, walking the various trails, with Jordan on the boat or Uncle Aiden and my dad doing reps in the pool. Long, carefree days spent in Port Albany. Next summer, I planned on working at BAM, so I was going to make the most of my final season.

Sitting on the beach, I saw Addi come out of her house and head my way. I waved at her as she approached. Her hair was down, rippling like gold in the sun, and she wore a pair of shorts and a T-shirt. As she grew closer, I couldn't help but notice how her T-shirt clung to her curves. I wasn't sure when she got those curves or how I'd missed noticing them. The way she walked made her hips sway—she looked sexy. My board shorts grew uncomfortably tight the closer she came, and I had to sit up, drawing my knees to my chest to hide my erection. I was confused and annoyed. It was Addi—my best friend. Why the hell was I reacting as if she was a girl?

She sat down, looking dejected. "Hey, Bray."

Reaching over, I ruffled her hair, noticing for the first time how silky the strands were against my fingers.

Was she using a different shampoo?

"Hey, little elf."

She huffed in annoyance. "Stop calling me that. I was six when I dressed up as an elf for Christmas."

I chuckled. "Addi, you still wear elf pajamas every year."

"Whatever." She tossed her head, clearly dismissing me, but her shoulders remained drooped, and she looked sad.

"What's wrong?"

"Todd broke up with me."

I felt two things at once. Relief and jealousy. I didn't like Todd. I used to until he'd asked Addi out, and after that, every time his name was mentioned, I found myself wanting to snarl and spit like some sort of demented dog.

"Good. He didn't deserve you."

She sighed, mimicking my pose and resting her chin on her hands. "He said I was too much work."

I snorted. "What a dick."

"Derek said the same thing—a couple weeks of dating me, and they were done." She looked at me, her wide blue eyes confused and upset. "What's wrong with me, Bray?"

I forgot everything in a second. My erection was gone, my confusion dissipated, and all that mattered was she was hurting and I had to help her. I scooted closer and wrapped my arm around her shoulders.

"Nothing is wrong with you, Addi. The problem is them. All they see is the outer package—how pretty you are. They aren't prepared for how incredibly clever your mind is. How you can talk circles around them. They have no idea how advanced you are." I snorted. "The reason they say you're too much work is they think with their dicks, not their minds." I shrugged when she gaped at me. "They aren't looking for a relationship, just to get laid." I held up my hands. "Only telling you the truth."

She gazed at me, and for a second, I saw Uncle Bent. Serious, determined, and older than her years. Then she began to giggle.

"You're awful."

"It's true, though."

She sighed and leaned into me. "I guess I'm just going to die alone, then."

It was my turn to laugh. "You're a little young for that, Addi. Give it some time. You need to find the right guy." I turned my head and kissed the top of her head. "You're too amazing to be alone forever."

A week later, I was in turmoil. Addi was suddenly everywhere. Everything about her was different. She was prettier, smarter, sexier. Her smiles taunted me. Her body tempted me. Her laughter was low and sultry.

I spent so much time in the cold water of the lake, even

my father was beginning to notice. Every time I would see Addi, my dick would spring up, and I had no choice but to escape to the water to settle him down. I started avoiding her, unsure what to do about my feelings and how they had changed toward her.

Unable to sleep one night, I padded down to the beach, listening to the sound of the water. The breeze was light and felt good on my bare chest, the sand cool under my toes as I walked. I leaned against a pile of rocks, admiring the moon hanging high in the sky. I startled when a soft voice broke through my thoughts.

"Couldn't sleep either?"

I turned and met Addi's eyes. She was sitting five feet from me, cross-legged on a large, flat rock. I had been so deep in thought, I hadn't even noticed her.

I noticed her now. Her hair was up, loose curls hanging around her face and shoulders. Her skin gleamed in the moonlight. She was wearing a baggy shirt and leggings, one shoulder bare. She was sexy and beautiful, and in that single moment, everything became clear. I was totally in love with her. I always had been. It was all I could do not to groan out loud.

"Uncle Bent know you're out here? Alone?" I asked, my voice low and gravelly, even to my own ears.

She shook her head. "He had to go back to the city. Mom is asleep. Everyone is. But I was restless." She shrugged. "I'm perfectly safe here, Brayden. Even Uncle Aiden admits that."

The grounds were protected with a private fence and gate.

There was a security system in place. I knew all that, and still, I didn't like it.

"No swimming alone," I snapped.

She huffed and scampered off the rocks, crossing her arms. "I'm not stupid, Bray. I know that." She shook her head. "I don't know what your problem is or why you're mad at me, but when you stop being a jerk, let me know."

She turned to leave, and I grabbed her arm, spinning her back to face me. I was shocked to see the tears in her eyes. "What? Why are you crying?"

"Why do you suddenly dislike me too? You've been avoiding me all week!"

"I don't dislike you," I replied. "That's the problem!"

"What?"

I didn't think; I only reacted. I yanked her into my arms and covered her mouth with mine and kissed her. She flung her arms around my neck and kissed me back. I slid my hands to cradle the back of her head, and deepened the kiss, groaning when her tongue touched mine. I lifted her to the rock, stepping between her legs, and for endless minutes, we explored each other. Learning and tasting. Our tongues stroked together, our breath mingling. I was aware of everything. How she fit against me. The subtle shiver that ran through her body as I touched her. The air surrounding us, the sound of the waves. How her nipples brushed against my chest. She fit against me seamlessly, melding against my chest. She tasted of chocolate and moonlight and all things Addi. It was a life-changing kiss for us both.

Breathing hard, I broke away. Our eyes met and held, hers wide and shocked, mine pleading and determined.

"I don't want you dating Todd or Derek or anybody else."

"Oh," she breathed out.

"You're mine, Addi. You have been your whole life. No one knows you the way I do. No one will ever understand you like me."

"But you've never…" She trailed off.

"I didn't know. Until this week. But it hit me. That's why I've hated every guy who looked at you twice. Why I go crazy thinking about someone else kissing you. Holding you. Because you're mine. You belong to me."

She swallowed, the tears spilling over her cheeks.

"What?" I asked again, wiping away the wetness. "Tell me."

She gripped my wrists, a shaky smile ghosting her lips.

"I thought you'd never figure it out."

Laughing, I kissed her again.

The next week was filled with ups and downs. I was on a high the next morning until I saw Addi on the beach. She looked pensive and upset.

"What's wrong?"

"We can't do this, Bray."

"Do what? We're not doing anything wrong," I insisted, yanking a hand through my hair.

"We're practically family. And I'm older than you."

I rolled my eyes with a snort. "By a little over a year. We grew up together, but we're not family in that sense, Addi.

We're not related in any way." I grabbed her hands. "Don't overthink this. We're perfect for each other."

She shook her head. "I need time to think."

That was never a good thing. Addi would think and analyze to the point we would never have a chance. She would talk herself out of this. Out of me.

In desperation, I went to Sandy—the adoptive grandmother of all of us. She had been the assistant to our fathers, her role growing and adapting as the years went by. She became their nucleus and had been part of our world our entire lives.

I confessed everything to her. My feelings. Addi's sudden hesitance and worry.

"Am I wrong, Nan? Am I wrong to have these feelings for her?"

She studied me. "Wrong? No. But have you thought of all the implications if this doesn't work out?"

"It will," I insisted. "Addi is mine. She always has been."

She smiled. "You sound just like your father."

"I know I'm young, but I see my whole life with her. As soon as I kissed her, I knew." I lifted my shoulder. "Maybe even before."

"What do you need, Brayden?"

"You know how she gets. Stubborn. She'll overthink and decide the risks are too great. She'll push me away."

"You want me to talk to her?"

"She'll listen to you, Nan. She always does."

I waited for two days. I was sitting on the rocks, watching the sun sparkle on the water. Addi lowered herself beside me.

"Hey."

I peered at her warily. "Hi."

"Nan called me over. We talked for a long time."

"And?"

She slipped her hand into mine. "Forgive me. I panicked."

Relief tore through me. "So, we're good?"

"She said a year was nothing, and I was being foolish."

"She's right."

"She told me she isn't shocked by this 'development'—" Addi used her fingers to make the quotations "—and that we're both more mature than most kids our age. She told me sometimes we're lucky and find our soul mates early. That what was important was how we felt, not what others would think."

"Ah," I murmured, hope beckoning.

"She told me to look in my heart." Addi squeezed my fingers. "She said that was where my future was, not in my head."

"Nan is a wise woman."

"I want to try."

"Then let's do it."

After talking to Addi and letting it settle for a few days, I spoke to my parents. It was a surprisingly short conversation. They weren't shocked, telling me they had seen it long before I did.

"We were waiting for you to make up your mind," my mother told me, cupping my face. "Your head had to catch up to your heart."

My dad had asked some good questions but informed me he wasn't really surprised about my feelings for Addi.

"You two have always had a bond." He paused. "But you need to come clean with Bent," he stated.

"I am. Tomorrow."

The next day, I paid a visit to Uncle Bentley and Auntie Emmy. My dad came with me for moral support.

Addi was sitting with her parents on their deck, drinking coffee, when my dad and I approached. I sat beside her, my hand finding hers under the table and squeezing her fingers. I swallowed nervously then met Uncle Bent's eyes. His expression was stern, his brow furrowed as he looked between us. Then he spoke.

"You are aware the table is glass and I can see that," he said, indicating our clasped hands.

I glanced down then began to laugh. I had forgotten that fact. Addi joined in my laughter, and I relaxed when the adults did as well.

"So, you're together now?" Emmy asked, smiling at us.

"Yes."

"Have you thought this out? What will happen if this doesn't work?" Bentley asked. "How it will affect everyone around you?"

My dad and Nan had asked the same question, so I wasn't surprised to hear him ask it as well. I drew in a deep breath before I responded.

"I'm young, Uncle Bent, not stupid. We talked about

that. But it's not going to happen." I met his serious gaze. "Addi is it for me."

"You're sixteen. She's a year ahead of you. What happens when she goes to university and you're still in high school?"

I shook my head. "I'm in advanced classes, Uncle Bent. I'll be going with her. And if we choose different schools, we'll figure it out." I didn't bother to tell him we already knew we would be going together.

Addi leaned forward. "You tell me all the time I'm like mom—young in years with an old soul."

Uncle Bentley's gaze grew warm, softening his stern look. "You are," he admitted.

"So is Brayden," my dad pointed out. "Come on, Bent, we always said this was going to happen. They've always been entwined. You can't possibly be surprised. It was inevitable."

He sighed and rubbed his eyes, then held up his hand. "Ground rules."

I bit back my grin. Uncle Bent always had ground rules.

He pointed at me. "You be careful. She's still young."

I felt myself flush, knowing exactly what he was saying.

"We're both too young," I mumbled. I knew we were both still virgins. For me, sex and love went hand in hand, and Addi was the same way. Although we had dated a few people, it had never gone that far for either of us.

"Good. Keep it that way until you're thirty—or even better, when I'm dead."

Auntie Emmy burst out laughing. "Stop it, Rigid. You're overreacting as usual. They're both good kids and plan to take this slow." She looked at us, one eyebrow lifted. "Right?"

We were both quick to agree.

"Same curfew and rules apply, Addi. I don't care whose son he is." He looked at me. "You pick her up and have her home at the set times. We prefer group outings. And no sneaking off while we're here.

"Same rules apply when we go back to Toronto. And when you start driving, you keep both hands on the wheel."

"Done." I had my learner's permit and planned on taking my test as soon as possible.

"You both will be respectful to us. Both your sets of parents. If we think things are getting too serious or you aren't following the rules, we're addressing it."

I agreed, nothing he said surprising me. I was actually shocked he didn't have more to say, but I had a feeling he would come to me later and talk to me privately. I also knew it was going to be far more personal and I wasn't going to enjoy it. But I would take it because it was for Addi.

"We're just starting, Uncle Bent. We wanted to be upfront with you. I don't want to hide anything or be deceitful." My parents were big on the truth and had drummed that into my head my whole life.

He smiled, some of the tension easing from his shoulders. "I appreciate that, Brayden." He met my gaze. "You take care of my little girl, and we won't have a problem. Otherwise…" He let the words trail off, then grinned. "I'll set Aiden on you."

"I will," I promised after the laughter had died down. I hunched closer, everyone else disappearing as I spoke directly

to him. "I care about her a lot, Uncle Bent. I won't hurt her. But seeing her with anyone else hurt me, so I had to speak up."

He clasped my shoulder with a firm nod. "I trust you, Brayden. If I didn't, you'd be in the lake by now." He winked. "We'll save that for another day." He squeezed hard in warning. "I'll be watching."

I sat back, relieved. Addi watched her father with amused adoration. He shook his finger at her. "You behave. You're too much like your mother."

She laughed. "Everyone says I'm like you."

"Then you'd be hitting the books, not mooning over Brayden."

She smirked and grinned. "I'm a woman. We can multitask."

He groaned. "Don't remind me."

I smiled at the memories. The years that followed. School, work, growing, and learning. Together. We were always together, and neither of us wanted it any other way. Ours wasn't a typical relationship. It never had been. Growing up together. Falling in love so young. We'd never been in a hurry to get married, because we knew how solid we were. We went to school, although Addi followed in Bentley's footsteps and left before she got her degree, with the same bug he possessed in that she was bored and was eager to enter the business world. I pushed and worked hard, and at twenty-five, I held my CPA degree. Addi was a young president at the age of twenty-six, but she had earned the title. Bentley was too smart a businessman to entrust the role to anyone who wasn't qualified—daughter or not.

And today was the day I'd been waiting for since I first kissed her. Our lives had settled enough that we could move on to the next step in our journey—husband and wife. We were ready.

Here in this place I loved. We had all our firsts here. First kiss. First declaration of our feelings. The first time we made love. The day I asked her to marry me. Our entire world was linked to this spot.

And it would continue. Our parents had gifted us a house here. BAM had slowly bought up every piece of land around the area. There was a bustling resort a couple of miles down the road run by a new division in the company. A successful winery run by another department—and where I would marry Addi today. The rest of the land was personal holdings of the company and its directors.

Our house was set away, still overlooking the water, close enough to the main area we were still part of the group, but with a little more privacy. A bluff was a natural wall with an easy access path toward the other grouping of houses. There was room by our place for three other houses—and more space behind us if needed. For some members of BAM, this was a fun place to escape, a weekend getaway, or a place to vacation. For others, it was our home.

I had lived here for a few months, while Addi divided her time between her parents' place in Toronto and here. Addi amused me with her objections to our living together before we got married, even when I reminded her both her parents and mine had done so.

"We're not them, Brayden," she replied, lifting her eyebrows.

"So old-fashioned, Addi," I teased back. "Let me get this straight. You'll stay with me in a house our parents gave us on weekends, but you won't live here until we're married."

She had tossed her hair. "The occasional weeknight as well."

I laughed. "Right. You realize that makes no sense, right?"

"It does to me."

I leaned close and kissed her. "Whatever makes you happy."

She cupped my cheek. "You do."

When she looked at me like that, and kissed me the way she did, I'd give her anything.

I always would.

CHAPTER 2
ADDISON

I woke up, throwing back the blankets and getting out of bed, regardless of the fact that the sun wasn't up yet. I threw on my favorite robe, added a wrap to my shoulders and stuffed my feet into a pair of warm socks. I always felt the cold—not the way my mom did, but more than most people. Layers were my friend. And strangely enough, my favorite season was winter. I had learned to dress properly and not let it stop me.

I headed downstairs, not bothering with lights. My feet knew the way, the incline of the stairs, the layout of the rooms I walked through. I pushed open the kitchen door, not at all surprised to find my dad sitting at the table, a pot of coffee at his elbow. His ever-present laptop was open, but he wasn't busy typing or reading emails. Instead, he sat at the table, staring out the window. The overhead light glinted on his dark hair, highlighting the shots of gray that were scattered throughout it. He was a handsome, distinguished man, his posture straight, his shoulders still broad. He worked out with my uncle Aiden daily and could easily run circles around my brother or cousins. Something he liked to do on the basketball court weekly.

I smiled at him, crossing the room. "Hi, Dad."

His return smile was tight. "Addi."

I grabbed a cup and held it out. He filled it for me, indicating a plate. "Your mom made you some cinnamon raisin scones last night. I knew you'd want them this morning."

I loved my mom's scones—especially the cinnamon raisin ones. I bent and kissed his cheek, sliding my arms around his neck for a hug. "Thanks."

He wrapped me in a fast embrace. "No problem."

I sat beside him, picking up a scone.

"You're up even earlier than I thought you'd be," he observed, taking a sip of coffee.

I peeked at the clock—it was barely after five.

"Big day."

He huffed into his cup. I studied him in the low light. He looked weary this morning. Still calm and unruffled—stoic and stern, but weary.

Bentley Ridge was a legend. He was known as a hard-nosed, brilliant businessman. Unflappable. Detached. His company, BAM, was synonymous with quality. What started out as a dream for him in college had grown beyond even his expectations. Together with my "uncles" Aiden Callaghan and Maddox Riley, they had built an empire. Land development, construction, office buildings, housing, house flips, and everything in between, they were known for their excellence. And now, the next generation, including Brayden and me, ran ABC, focused on the outskirts of Toronto and finding new income streams, concentrating on the commercial aspects. A successful resort, a winery I had rescued from ruin, and a small private grouping of retirement cottages were some of our most profitable triumphs so far.

I was often compared to my father. I had inherited his business acumen and his stern resting face. While other little girls were playing with dolls, I sat on my dad's knee, listening and learning. I was known as severe and humorless. Emotionless. I had been referred to often as "a chip off the old block." Strangely enough, that comparison didn't bother me at all. I considered it a compliment. Like my father, I didn't much care what the business world thought of me personally. I let my record speak for itself.

But the faces we showed the world and those we showed the people we loved were vastly different. My dad was one of the kindest, generous, and most loving men in the world. Behind closed doors, with his family and those he treasured, he smiled and laughed. Teased and cajoled. Thought nothing of getting on the floor and wrestling my siblings or giving me a piggyback ride when we were younger. Sitting beside us, explaining homework and helping us understand. His patience with us always amazed me, given his cut-and-dried persona with business. With his extended family, he showed the same love and caring. He was loyal and protective. Always ready to help out or offer encouragement.

His adoration for my mother hadn't diminished over the years. Their love was a constant, steady light—a beacon for me and an example I wanted to live by. They still looked at each other with love and lit up when the other would enter a room. My father fussed over my mom, constantly bringing her gifts of soft shawls or fuzzy socks to keep her warm. Every floor in the house had been redone with radiant heating—he couldn't bear to see her cold. She watched over him zealously, accepting his need to care for her easily, knowing how much it meant to him. She made him smile, even on the darkest days, and reminded him, more than once, life and family came first.

The same lesson she drummed into our heads.

I touched his hand. "You okay, Dad?"

He smiled. "Of course."

"You look tired. I'm getting married today. You should be happy." He'd seemed fine when I went up to bed last night. "You're finally getting rid of me. All that is left is Chloe and you'll have the place to yourself again."

He sighed and flipped his hand over, encasing mine. "Forgive my moroseness, my girl. It hit me after you went to bed, it would be the last night I had you under my roof. Still mine to look after. As of today, Brayden will be the one who cares for you." I was shocked to see the glimmer of tears in his eyes. "Your home will be with him."

"Daddy," I whispered, the childish word slipping out.

"I walked the house all night, thinking—remembering. The day you were born and we brought you home. I was terrified. You were so small and helpless, and you needed me so much. I was so sure I would mess it up. But your mother told me I was being ridiculous, and as usual, she was right. I learned all of it. The diapers, the feedings, the tricks of surviving on no sleep and endless parades up and down the halls when you wouldn't settle." He paused. "I used to snuggle you right here—" he patted his shoulder "—in the crook on my neck and hum and walk. Sometimes it was the only thing that soothed you."

I squeezed his fingers.

"I watched you grow from a baby into this incredible young woman sitting in front of me, Addi. I cheered every accomplishment and success, even though I knew each one was a step that took you further away from me." He shook his head. "I am so incredibly proud of you—of the person you are, the businesswoman you've become." His voice caught. "I'll miss having you here."

"You didn't get this emotional when Thomas moved out." My brother had gone to university in BC, studying to become a marine biologist. He was still in school, working on his master's and had plans to pursue his PhD. He came home on occasion, hardly looking like the baby brother who had left when he was eighteen. My parents flew out regularly to see him, and we kept in contact via text and phone.

He smiled, lifting a shoulder. "That was different. You're my baby girl. My firstborn."

"And Chloe is still here," I reminded him. My younger sister eschewed anything to do with the business world. Her love was animals, and she was in school to become a veterinarian assistant. She lived at home; although her hours were so crazy, I rarely saw her anymore.

He smiled. "Not for much longer, I think. She graduates soon and has her eye on a clinic in Burlington. She's getting ready to fly on her own, as she should be. I'll suffer then too." He paused. "All my children—gone from my house. It's too fast."

I was out of my chair in a second. My dad caught me and pulled me into his lap, hugging me. It was rare for him to be this emotional. I snuggled my head onto his shoulder, feeling the strength of his embrace and the warmth of his love surround me.

"It's been a long time since you sat on my lap," he chuckled.

"I think I used to fit better."

He held me closer. "You fit perfectly." He kissed my head. "I want you to be happy, Addi. It's all I ever wanted for you."

"Brayden makes me happy, Dad. He loves me so much." I plucked at the sleeve of his heavy sweatshirt. "I love him. He gets me."

"I know," he sighed, resting his chin on my head. "That is the only reason I can do this. You two were always meant for each other." I felt the press of his lips on my forehead. "Forgive your old dad, Addi. Today is a happy day, and I'm thrilled. Brayden is going to take good care of my little girl, and you're going to have a wonderful life together." He hugged me again and released me. I slid to my chair, wiping my eyes.

"Promise me you'll save me a dance or two."

"Always."

"Be happy, Addi. And if you ever need me—I'm right here."

"I'll always need you."

"Brayden is going to step into my shoes. In many ways, he already has. He'll watch over you and be your protector." He smiled ruefully. "Just like you will be for him. But I'll be watching, and I'll be right here. Always. You always have a place here." He squeezed my hand. "Not that I expect you ever to need it. Your mother and I love him like one of our own, and despite my silly emotions of the moment, I am overjoyed for you."

"I kinda like your silly emotions."

"Your mother will kick my ass and withhold scones if she thinks I've upset you on your wedding day."

I grinned. My father fell in love with my mother and her scones simultaneously. She was tiny but fierce, and most people would be shocked to know who the real boss was in the household. My father deferred to her in most things, always saying she was smarter than he was by far.

"You haven't upset me, Dad. I like knowing how much you love me."

"I do."

I winked. "That's my line today."

He laughed. "So it is." He slid a box my way. "For you, my girl."

I opened the slim box, unable to hide my tears. A delicate bracelet lay on the satin, the white gold shimmering in the low light. A small heart embraced a pearl, creamy pink and pale. The tiniest of diamonds highlighted the curve of the heart. I knew that pearl. It was one that belonged to my grandmother—one of the few precious items my dad had of hers. Its mates were worn around my mother's neck—she rarely took off the necklace. As a child, I was fascinated with them. The smooth texture, the pretty color, the way they glimmered in the light. My mother let me touch them, quietly telling me how precious they were and that I had to be careful. I would trace them with the greatest of reverence. When I was older and knew the story behind them, my love for them, and my father, only grew.

"Dad," I breathed.

"Your mom thought you should have one of the pearls. We redesigned her necklace and had this made. We know you prefer bracelets to necklaces." He leaned over and helped me put it on.

"I'll never take it off."

He smiled. "It's your something old for today, Addi. Besides me walking you down the aisle."

I laughed as I wiped away my tears.

"Thank you."

He leaned close and pressed his lips to my cheek.

"Love you, baby girl."

My breath caught. "I love you, Daddy."

He winked. "I know."

The sounds of laughter and gaiety filled the room. I looked in the mirror at the cluster of women around me, smiling as I took a sip of champagne. I met my sister's eyes in the reflection, and she winked, knowing what I was thinking.

How incredibly lucky we were to be surrounded by these amazing women.

The winery had been designed to accommodate weddings and other events. I discovered it one day while out with Gracie. The wine was superb, but the land underutilized, the main building crumbling, and the business dying. ABC purchased it, kept the people who knew about wine, and demolished and rebuilt the rest. When I saw the designs, I knew it was where I wanted to get married, and we had, in fact, deferred our wedding until it was ready. The room I was in was on the top floor, facing the water, the wide sweep of windows showing the waves as they danced in the afternoon sun, the scattering of snowflakes delicate and beautiful amid the wildness of the water.

My mom sat on the sofa, a glass of wine in her hand, her golden hair catching the light. She was laughing at something Cami said, her head thrown back in amusement. She was a tiny dynamo, the center of my father's world, the rock for my siblings and me. She was always there, a constant in my life, my father by her side. Every school event, outside activity, achievement, victory, punishment—they handled together—for my siblings and me. They were hands-on, dedicated, loving parents. I knew we were wealthy, but we weren't spoiled. We earned our allowance, followed the rules, and acted like kids. My mother often joined in on the antics and dragged my father with her.

There was no doubt who the free spirit in the relationship was.

She was sitting with Cami and Dee, Becca, Liv, Fee, Katy, and of course, my Nan, Sandy. A close-knit group of women, strong, fierce, and the role models I tried to live up to. All were special, all a significant part of my life. Aunts in name only, they were as close to me as if joined by blood. So were their offspring.

Flitting around the room were my attendants. Shelby, Brayden's sister; Ava, Aiden's daughter; and Heather, Richard's younger daughter, were checking on gowns, chatting, helping one another with their hair. We didn't want stylists or makeup artists with us today. It was all about family, so we were spending the hours before my wedding together. The only one missing was Grace, Richard's eldest daughter and my best friend.

I frowned at my sister. "Chloe, where is Gracie? She should be here by now."

Chloe shrugged, glancing over her shoulder. "Hey, Hedda," she called, using an old nickname, "Where is your sister?"

Heather picked up her phone. "She's en route."

Katy VanRyan, her mom, frowned. "She's cutting it close. That's not like Gracie."

Heather poured some more champagne. "I think this case has her distracted. Something has."

She stood and came over to the small area we had called the salon. She bent to pour some more champagne in my glass, keeping her voice low. "Her text says she's bringing a plus-one and she hopes that's okay." She snorted delicately. "She says you don't have to feed him. Stick a chair outside for him, I think was her quote."

I lifted my eyebrows. "*Him*? Gracie is bringing a date?" I whispered. Gracie never had time to date. She was too busy with her career.

Heather looked perturbed. "She hasn't said anything to me until now. I'm as shocked as you."

"We'll have to grill her," Chloe muttered.

I laughed. "That'll produce nothing. You know how intensely private she is. We'll have to sic Nan on her."

If anyone could get Gracie to talk, it would be Sandy.

Cami stood, cinching the belt on her robe. Her dark hair was swept into an elegant chignon, and her face was youthful, the small lines around her eyes only evident when she smiled. She clapped her hands. "Girls, you need to get dressed." She met my eyes. "And we need to get you into your gown."

I looked at the elegant, gossamer dress hanging in the window, designed and made by Cami. She had done the girls' dresses as well. The bodice of my dress was tight-fitting, heavily beaded with shimmering pearls and crystals. Strapless, it clung to me like a second skin. The bottom was layers of ivory tulle that burst forth from my waist like a cloud of air. Delicate flowers were embroidered on the skirt. Brayden was going to love it. I could already picture his smile as I walked toward him. The way he would bend low and whisper how beautiful I was. The way his eyes would glow. How his voice would deepen as he told me he looked forward to getting me out of my dress later.

I felt my cheeks flush simply at the thought.

Hanging beside my dress was a thick, knitted ivory sweater with matching mitts and a pair of ivory, faux fur-lined ankle boots. A matching sweater hung in Brayden's closet.

Because ours was not a traditional wedding. No church, no long ceremony or wait time between the wedding and reception. No gifts—we'd asked our guests to donate to a local animal shelter instead.

We were getting married downstairs in a room filled with garlands, trees, lights, music, and flowers. Surrounded by our family and closest friends. Then, thanks to the staff and the muscle of all the boys, Brayden and I would don our heavy sweaters and boots and would have our pictures taken outside surrounded by the woods and snow. They had cleared a couple of areas so the pictures would be lovely.

Brayden and I loved everything about this place and this season. Skiing, skating, walking in the snow. Snowball fights and cold noses. We wanted the winter backdrop, and it was the winery's manager who suggested the two areas for pictures of the two of us. The rest, including family pictures, would be inside, although my mother insisted she wanted a couple done outdoors.

My father had looked askance at the idea, reminding her of how easily she got cold. In reply, she shook her head, laughing. "Relax, Rigid. I often sit by the fire pit in the winter. And we go for walks."

"Not in a dress," he argued.

"It's for a couple of pictures. I think they'll be charming." She leaned close to him, brushing her lips on his cheek. "If I get cold, you can warm me up."

He turned his head, kissing her hard. "I will." He looked at me. "You get a few pictures fast, and then she goes back inside."

"Done." I chuckled over their exchange. I was used to their displays of affection and my father's overprotectiveness with her.

Chloe interrupted my musings, setting down a box beside me. "Jen brought the flowers. Here's your headpiece."

"Where is he?" I asked, anxious to see him. The eccentric wedding planner would make sure everything was in place for me.

"Downstairs, checking on everything. He's in his element down there." She grinned. "Dressed to the nines as usual, bossing them all around. He says he will be up shortly."

I laughed. Jen had come into my parents' lives when they were getting married and had become a member of the family. Outrageous with his own style, he was elegant and perfect with details for events. It was he who suggested the color of the dresses for the girls, insisting the red and green would be so "cliché." He had been right, and the color scheme of ivory and gold, with punches of red and green, was beautiful. Each girl had a dress designed especially for her, and Cami had done an exquisite job. The boys would all be in simple black tuxes, their ties and cummerbunds a striped combination of the ivory and gold. I loved all of it.

I opened the box with eager fingers, and Chloe settled the circlet around my head. It matched the bouquets and decorations everywhere. Holly, ivy, sprigs of balsam and cedar, entwined with red roses, tiny pinecones, and white freesias. My headpiece had a few crystals to match my dress woven into the greens. Chloe skillfully pinned the headpiece and stood back, nodding happily.

"There. You're ready."

My hair, the same golden wheat color as my mother's, hung in loose curls over my shoulders. Chloe had woven some pearls and sparkles into the front, and the headpiece looked pretty. I smiled at my sister as she bent down, laying her head alongside mine. Our facial features were similar, but other than that, I had my mother's coloring with my dad's blue eyes. Chloe had my dad's hair and my mom's wide, dark eyes. We were both small like my mom. Our brother, Thomas, had my dad's height, coloring, and his eyes.

"If you decide the vet helper thing isn't your calling, you could always fall back on hairdressing," I teased.

She winked. “I'll keep that in mind.”

The door opened, and Gracie stumbled in, dragging a suitcase. Her dark hair was a mess, her usually calm blue eyes filled with panic. Her coat was half buttoned, and her cheeks were flushed.

“Oh my god! I made it.” She dropped her bag, shrugging off her coat, hugging and kissing everyone. “I'm so sorry!” She made a beeline for me, and I stood and hugged my best friend. Though she was older than me by a couple of years, Gracie and I had always been close.

“Thank god.” I held her fiercely. “The day wouldn't have been right without you.”

“Not happening. A bad engine, a delayed take-off, a snowstorm—nothing was keeping me from being here.”

I studied her closely. “Are you okay, Grace? You look frazzled.”

Grace never looked frazzled. She always had everything under control.

She waved me off. “I've been running since yesterday, trying to get here.” She accepted a glass of champagne from Heather, downing it in one long tip of her head. “I need another one of those.”

I met Heather's shocked gaze. I had never seen Grace drink like that. Small, measured sips were all she ever took. I noticed a couple other things. A patch or two of pink on her neck as if she'd rubbed against something rough. A tiny bruise not quite hidden by the collar of her blouse. The brightness of her eyes. I held back a gasp when I noticed her finger. There was a thin pink line on her left ring finger. Her wedding ring finger. It looked as if a band had been there, then removed recently.

"Grace," I whispered. "What's going on?"

She ignored my words. "I'm here to see my best friend get married."

"We're going to talk about this," I hissed.

"Not today," she said, keeping her smile wide and her words low. "Today is about you."

"Just tell me you're okay."

She pressed a kiss to my cheek. "I promise."

I had to take her word for it since we had no time to delve deeper. But I had to ask.

"Who is the plus-one?"

She rolled her eyes. "A necessary pain in my ass. But I owe him for getting me here, and he wanted to come to the wedding. I hope it's okay." Her words were simple, but I noticed her cheeks flushed as she spoke.

"It's fine. You know we're casual."

"Thanks."

Our conversation was interrupted when Cami clapped her hands together again. "Girls, it's time."

"I need a fast shower," Grace insisted, wrinkling her nose. "I smell like I've been travelling for days."

Her mother stood. "Come, and I'll show you where."

I watched her walk away, trying to tamp down my curiosity. She hadn't smelled like she'd been travelling to me. She smelled like a man had been all over her. The scent was deep—citrusy and musky. Gracie's fragrance was very light and floral.

My curiosity grew, and I was suddenly anxious to meet her plus-one.

CHAPTER 3

BRAYDEN

My dad showed up a short time later in the morning, along with Aiden and Bentley. Although in my mind they were still my uncles, I had begun using their first names once I started working at BAM. When Addi and I got engaged, we had talked to Bentley about the whole Mom and Dad thing, and we agreed to stick to names. Since our parents spent so much time together, it would have become confusing. Bentley knew what he meant to me. So did Aiden. They were as close to me as I was to my own dad, and I was grateful to have three such strong men as role models. We walked over to the Hub, the morning air crisp and cold. It was a massive building we all used for various things. It had a full gym, a basketball court, a games area, as well as three bowling lanes in the large, high-ceilinged basement. Upstairs was a wide-open space with an attached fully outfitted kitchen that we used for our gatherings. A glassed-in swimming pool for the winter that overlooked the lake and a huge movie room were on the main floor. It had been well-planned and thought-out. There was a little library at the back next to the pool, filled with books and comfortable chairs. My mom often sat there reading, with Emmy or Cami for company.

We hadn't even poured coffee yet when Richard VanRyan, Van, Halton, and Reid showed up. A few moments later, Jordan, or Pops as we called him, strolled in, dragging the Callaghan boys, Theo, Thomas, and Reed.

My tribe was all here. We had way more adopted "cousins" than we could fit into a wedding party, but they would all be in attendance and all had a job. We needed ushers, drivers for guests, various errands run for the wedding party—and the group all happily volunteered, and we considered them as much a part of our day as the ones standing beside us at the altar.

We hadn't wanted stag or doe parties, so the younger members of the group hosted a party for us here last night. We laughed, drank, ate, and danced, no parents or grandparents allowed. We sent them all out to dinner at their favorite place in Toronto, and they hosted some of the out-of-town guests. They enjoyed themselves, we cut loose, and everyone was happy. Hardly traditional, but Addi and I were anything but.

A wedding days before Christmas, pictures outside, a two-night honeymoon in our own home, followed by a full-blown BAM Christmas? Most women would have refused, but the entire thing was my Addi's idea.

Which was why she was perfect for me.

A hand on my shoulder broke my thoughts. My dad's warm blue gaze met mine. "Quit daydreaming, son. You'll be at the altar soon enough. We've got breakfast, some basketball, and a bunch of work to do."

I grinned. "I'm looking forward to the altar the most."

He chuckled. "I know. I felt the same way the day I married your mother."

"We all felt that way," Bentley said, adding a couple of scones to his plate. Everything else had been catered, but the scones came from Emmy. He wouldn't eat any others.

Bentley clapped my arm as he went by. "Knowing my Addi, she's as anxious as you. Emmy said she was enjoying her girl time, so you need to enjoy us."

I snorted. "They sit around, have their nails done, drink, and discuss us." I grinned widely. "They conspire together on how to keep us in line. All we do is work and let you old-timers beat us at basketball on occasion."

"Hey, who you calling old?" Aiden protested,

flexing his muscles. "I can beat you—all of you—with one hand tied behind my back."

I smirked. Aiden was still huge. Tall, his posture ramrod straight. He worked out daily and could tire me out most of the time. His hair was completely gray now, with silver woven into the strands, and his scruff matched. But he was strong and agile, and he made sure we all were as well.

Like a single unit, Ronan, Paul, and Jeremy all stopped shoveling food into their mouths and looked up. Aiden's triplets weren't identical, but they were similar, all taking after Aiden in their size and looks. Dark-haired with green eyes, they were large and liked to work out and do most things together.

"You're on, old man," Ronan teased, always the spokesman for the group. The boys all high-fived one another, tilting their chins toward their father in a threatening way that made me laugh. Aiden narrowed his eyes.

"You're going down, son."

"Which one?" They spoke in unison.

"All of you." He jerked his head toward Bentley and Maddox. "I got my boys."

"Hey," Richard interjected. "I'll get in on that."

Ronan chuckled. "The three of us will take on all of you—except Pops. He's ours."

Everyone laughed as Jordan rolled his shoulders. "You heard them, gents. I'm the ace in the hole."

"That you are, Pops," hooted Reed.

The rest of the meal was filled with taunts and general ribbing. The breakfast disappeared as if none of them had seen food in months, leaving Bentley shaking his head. "I ordered double what I thought we needed." But he didn't look surprised.

After breakfast, we divided into teams and hit the court in the basement. There was a lot of trash-talking, unnecessary roughhousing, and taunts. Aiden took on his triplets, his eldest son, Liam, adding himself to his dad's team, and they held their own, although they had to admit defeat. The triplets were like a well-oiled machine, knowing one another's moves before they happened. You could never win if they weren't on your team. Still, it was fun to watch.

My dad got my attention. "We need to get you ready. Our tuxes are at your place. Everyone will get ready at their own homes and meet back here. The cars will drive us over."

"Jen with the girls?"

He smirked. "His favorite place to be. I think he arrived with the flowers and was making sure everything was perfect. We'll have to pass his inspection before he lets us in the building."

I laughed. The quirky male wedding coordinator was part of every celebration we ever had, as well as many family functions. He was outrageous, droll, and his eccentricity had only become more so as he aged. He walked with a cane now and only worked on select, personal weddings. He had been a huge help for ours.

I glanced at my watch, knowing in three hours I would be meeting Addi at the altar. I could hardly wait.

"Let's do this."

I came out of my room, pulling on my bow tie. "Dad, I need help."

He laughed, standing up and approaching me. His once silver hair was now pure white, and his laugh lines were deep around his eyes and mouth. But his back was straight, his shoulders broad, and he was strong. We had a close relationship. My mother said I was him made over except for my eyes, which were like hers. I did bear a strong resemblance to him, although I liked to tease him and say I was better-looking.

He was a great father, always there for Shelby and me. He was endlessly patient, never raised his voice, and was fiercely protective. He had been thrilled when I developed my love of numbers, encouraging me and helping me every step of the way. He'd been so proud when I graduated early and continued on to become a certified accountant like him. Shelby was the exact opposite—a dreamer and artistic to the core. She painted and drew, her fingers constantly covered in paint and ink. Her room was too until Dad had Van build her a little studio in the BAM building, where she happily spent most of her time after she left school. She worked at a local gallery, surrounded by art, and dedicated the rest of her time to creating.

He straightened the ends of the fabric with a shake of his head. "You have never got the hang of this."

"Didn't need to," I quipped. "I had you."

His hands stilled, and he met my eyes. His light blue shimmered, and he blinked. "You always will, Brayden."

I was shocked at the emotion on his face and in his voice. My dad gave us lots of hugs and always told us how much he loved us, how proud he was, but other than rare occasions, he kept his emotions hidden. I knew he shared them openly with my mother, but it was uncommon to see a crack in his façade.

I laid a hand on his shoulder. "I know, Dad. You have always been there for me."

He nodded, looking over my shoulder. "I never had that growing up, and I wanted to make sure you knew how important you were—you are—to me."

I knew about his childhood. When I was old enough, he had told me. He was worried he wasn't a good enough dad, but I hadn't lied when I told him I couldn't have a better one. Maddox Riley was everything I wanted to be for my own kids. Strong, loving, and generous. I wanted to be the kind of husband he was to my mother. I wanted Addi to look at me years down the road and know she was as important to me then as she was when we began. More so, even. My parents' relationship, although not perfect, was strong and unbreakable. They laughed and loved, fought and cried. Made up and carried on. Devoted themselves to each other and to us.

"I do know, Dad. You've always told me how much you loved me."

He cleared his throat, but the words were still choked.

"I know wedding days are mostly about the bride. Bentley is having an inner meltdown over Addi getting married today." He tried to smile, but his lips trembled. "But I am as well. You're my boy, Brayden. Something I did right from the moment you were born."

He didn't let me say anything. "I wanted to give you something today. Impart wisdom and sage advice, but to be honest, you don't need it. You're amazing, son. You're loving and giving. Your mother and I are incredibly proud of the man you've become."

I felt tears gather at his words.

"Bentley gave Addi something today for her old. Something that meant a great deal to him. Again, I know it's the bride's tradition, but I wanted to give you something as well. Something as precious to me as you are." He sucked in a deep breath. "Something for your future I hope you'll use."

I couldn't speak. My throat was too thick, so I nodded.

He tilted his chin, and I turned, noticing something I hadn't until now.

A small lamp I recalled from my childhood was sitting on the counter. I'd learned the history of it as I got older, finally understanding the reason it was so special to my father. A broken piece of his childhood my mother had restored. It sat in the nursery when I was a child, and I often touched the paint, gazing at the truck and the streetlight that stood over it, almost protecting it.

My dad would use it every night as he read to me. Turned it on when I was scared, to comfort me. Take off the shade and make hand puppets in the light thrown against the wall. It was always there when I was growing up.

The same way he was.

I met his gaze, not bothering to wipe the tears off my cheek.

"For your son," he said. "Or daughter."

Shelby never liked it. She preferred girlie things. Once I grew older, the lamp disappeared from the nursery and sat high on a shelf in his office. Protected.

And now, he was giving it to me. A symbol of his past so dear to him, I knew right then how deeply he loved me. More than I had ever imagined him doing. That was the real gift.

I embraced him, suddenly six years old again. Seeking his strength and warmth, which he gave freely. We stood for long moments, the love in the room tangible and rich. Then he stepped back and clapped his hands on my shoulders, letting me see his emotions.

"Be happy, Bray," he murmured.

"I will. I love her, Dad."

"I know. You'll be a great partner for Addi. You were meant to be together."

I nodded. He was right. She was my soul mate.

I indicated the lamp. "I'll take good care of it."

He smiled. "I know. I look forward to reading to my grandson with it."

"I'll get right on that."

He threw back his head, the moment lighter.

"I'll keep that to myself."

For a moment, our eyes locked, and I knew I would never forget this moment with my dad.

He squeezed my shoulders. "Let's go get you married."

"Sounds good."

CHAPTER 4
ADDISON

My stomach fluttered with nerves as I stepped into the cloud of tulle and lace. Cami slipped the dress up, making quick work of the hidden zipper and covered buttons that graced the back of the gown. I drew in a deep breath as the boning cinched in, and I ran my finger over the scalloped edge of the beading that hugged my breasts.

"This isn't going anywhere."

Cami met my eyes in the mirror, winking. "I'm sure Brayden will consider it a challenge later. Tell him to be gentle. I worked hard on this one."

My breath caught as I looked in the mirror. "You've outdone yourself," I whispered in awe. "It's beautiful."

"*You're* beautiful," Cami replied.

I felt like a princess or a fairy queen. The skirt billowed out around me, the sparkles catching the light. I never considered myself particularly beautiful. Brayden insisted I was, and the way he looked at me made me feel special and beautiful in his eyes, and that was enough. My dad called me lovely all the time and my mom insisted I was as well, but I always thought it was because they, like Brayden, looked at me with love. I was just me. Nothing special.

But today, in this dress, I felt beautiful.

My mom stepped behind the divider, her hand flying to her mouth. Tears filled her eyes. "Addi," she breathed out. "Oh, your father is going to lose it when he sees you."

"You as well, Mom. You look gorgeous."

She smiled and stepped close, laying her head along mine. Her golden hair was interwoven with silver, highlighting the color. She refused to have it dyed, and my father loved it. It was gathered in an elegant braid that hung down her back, laced with sparkles and ribbon. Her dress, a rich green, suited her coloring. It was long-sleeved, cinched tight at the waist, the sweetheart neckline showing off her throat and the redesigned necklace she wore. She was elegant and beautiful.

She kissed my cheek. "We'll both wow him."

Chloe slipped in, grinning. Her dress shimmered in the lights, the soft gold creation perfect on her. "Dad is going to blubber like a baby when he sees us. He's already emotional."

My mom smiled. "Your dad is having a hard

time that his baby is getting married and her sister probably not far behind."

Chloe rolled her eyes. "I'm too busy for a man. I plan on staying at home until I'm fifty. Rent is cheap. My laundry is done, and the food is good." She winked. "And dad has a driver for me, and he lets me shop. Why do I need another man?"

We all laughed. Chloe loved all the benefits of living at home, including the car and driver Dad had at her disposal. He always worried with the hours she kept that she would fall asleep at the wheel, or worse yet, get mugged on a subway or bus. She had resisted at first, then decided she liked it. As for the rest—I couldn't argue. She did, on occasion, do her own laundry, and I knew my dad gave her a budget for her "shopping," although I was certain it was generous. Otherwise, she had it nailed. Our parents had been the same with all of us, including paying for our education. They insisted they wanted us to concentrate on studying, not having to juggle jobs and school. My mother had done it on her own, and my father didn't want us having to go through what she had, struggling to keep up.

"Not my children," he vowed. "I worked hard to make your life easier, so indulge me."

And we did.

I was grateful—we all were—we knew how lucky we were to have Bentley Ridge as our father.

Mom smiled. "He will be very proud."

She hugged us, and we stepped out from behind the screen. I gasped in delight at the girls. All in varying tones from cream and ivory to soft gold and their dresses styled to suit them, they were beautiful. The bouquets matched my headpiece, and each had a little piece of festiveness in her hair—a spray of holly, some ivy, the glitter of sparkles—some tiny sprig of the theme. They brought tears to my eyes.

They all loved my dress, oohing and aahing at Cami's creation. Jen came forward, clucking as he fixed the hem, fussed with my headpiece, and tamed a stray lock of hair back into place.

"A masterpiece of loveliness." He glanced over my shoulder. "Cami, you have done yourself proud. The entire wedding party is perfect."

She hummed her thanks, smiling widely.

I leaned close. "Is he here? Has Brayden arrived?"

Jen smiled, his eyes soft. "Your groom is waiting anxiously downstairs for you." He looked at Chloe. "You have the ring?"

She nodded, sliding her fingers into the hidden pocket added just for that reason. "Yep."

He turned to the group. "Remember. Slow and graceful. I don't want anyone charging down the aisle." He threw me a wink. "Even you. Once you get an eyeful of your man, you might want to, but don't. Enjoy the walk. Take in the splendor the room has become. The ambiance is—" he paused and brought his fingers to his lips in a kiss "—pure romance."

I nodded, my nerves easing a bit now I knew Brayden was here. Not that there had been any doubts, but somehow, I relaxed more knowing he was in the building. I fiddled with my bracelet, sliding my finger over the smooth surface of the pearl. My mom noticed and smiled. Then she slipped a small box into my hand.

"Your groom asked me to give this to you."

I held my breath as I opened the box. A set of earrings, pearls so similar to the one my dad gave me this morning, were nestled in dark velvet. They were surrounded by tiny diamonds that twinkled in the light. Delicate and elegant, they could be worn any time, but for today, they would be special. Brayden knew me so well. There was a small note, and I plucked it from the top.

Wear for me. I love you. B

I stifled a sob, and Mom helped me put them in. She nodded.

"Perfect. He chose well."

"I think he had help."

She smiled. "He and your father may have had a talk. But the idea was his."

"Did he get his cuff links?"

"Yes. He loved them."

I drew in a deep breath and glanced at the clock.

"Oh god, ten minutes," I whispered.

My mom slipped her fingers under my chin. "Are you ready?"

"Yes."

Jen lifted his arms. "Then, ladies, in your positions. We're heading down to the back room now." He looked at me. "I'll send your father up in five. I'll get the girls in order. You'll be at the back. I'll send them down at the right moment."

"My sweater…" I asked, suddenly anxious.

"I will have it for afterward. Everything is handled." His smile was wide. "All you have to do is be the bride. We've got the rest covered." He handed me my bouquet. "All right?"

"Yes."

I waited, listening for my father's footsteps. When he appeared, he was silent, staring at me for a moment. His eyes misted over, and he wiped at his face, not at all embarrassed by his emotions. He leaned down and kissed my cheek, his voice thick. "The last time I saw a bride this beautiful, it was your mother."

"Thanks, Dad."

"Brayden is going out of his skin, waiting for you." He smiled, although his eyes were watery. "It's time to take you to him."

"Please."

He tucked my arm into his. "You sure you don't

want to duck and run? We could go get ice cream." He winked, letting me know he was joking.

"Maybe after."

"Anytime, Addi. Anything, anytime."

I squeezed his arm. "I know."

He sighed. "Then let's get you married."

I peeked through the door before the girls started their walk. The room was resplendent. The glow of candles, the scent of pine and roses, the garlands and trees twinkling with lights. I spied the groomsmen, dashing in their tuxes, waiting patiently. Ronan, Paul, and Jeremy all stood out, their broad shoulders towering over everyone. Thomas was smiling at something Liam said as they sat down, their usher duties done. Beside Brayden was Reed, standing proud, his hand on Brayden's shoulder.

My breath caught at the sight of him. Tall, his shoulders straight, his hands crossed in front of him, looking anxious, was my Brayden. The light glinted off his light-brown hair, carefully brushed and gleaming. His chiseled jaw was smooth, and his tux fit him perfectly. He was built lean like his father, but his clothes hid the perfection of his taut torso, muscular biceps, and toned body. I knew those muscles all too well. How they felt under my fingers, the way they rippled as we made love.

His verdant green eyes were fixed on the aisle.

Waiting for me. As anxious as I was to become united as one.

The music swelled, and Jen spread his arms.

"Ladies, it's time."

BRAYDEN

I tugged on my sleeves, the new cuff links that had been waiting for me when I got here making me smile. Like my father, I enjoyed dressing up, and cuff links were something I liked to collect. These were amazing, inlaid with mother-of-pearl and a small sapphire the color of Addi's eyes in the center. They were now my favorite pair, and I would think of this day every time I wore them.

I tried to concentrate on the girls as they drifted by, each one lovely, their gowns no doubt perfect. But I only had eyes for one woman today. And when she appeared, she took my breath away.

Far too slowly, she came down the aisle, her arm tucked into Bentley's, his hand covering hers. It took all I had to stay in place, not to meet her partway down the flower-strewn carpet and pull her from her father and into my arms.

Had she ever been more beautiful?

Her hair tumbled over her bare shoulders, the pretty circlet on her head making me smile. Her breasts were high, set off with the ivory material.

Her skin shimmered in the muted lighting. She didn't walk; she glided. Glints of beads and crystals reflected around her. Her full skirt seemed to float, diaphanous and delicate. She was a vision.

And her eyes. Her beautiful eyes were focused on me as intensely as mine were on her. The blue glimmered and shone, her love clearly written in her expression. My heartbeat picked up, and I had to remind myself this wasn't a dream. This woman would be mine now. Mine to love, to care for, and to hold. Forever.

I stepped forward as they reached the evergreen-covered arbor and held out my hand, shaking Bentley's and waiting as he kissed Addi's cheek, then transferred her hand to mine. I felt his reluctance. I saw how his hand shook, and I knew how deeply emotional this moment was for him. How much she meant to him.

"I will guard her with my life," I murmured for his ears only. "You never have to worry about her happiness."

He met my gaze and squeezed my shoulder. "I know."

He moved to sit by Emmy, who reached for his hand. He covered hers with both of his and leaned forward, brushing his mouth over hers. It was a moment of love between them, and I wondered how I would feel years ahead when it was my turn.

I gazed down at Addi. I couldn't move until I told her. "You are exquisite," I whispered to her.

"You're not so bad yourself."

"Ready to do this, little elf?"

"You lead, I'll follow," she replied quietly.

"How about we do it together?"

"Even better."

The ceremony was simple and uncomplicated. Short. Neither of us wanted a long, drawn-out affair. We stated the vows we had written for each other, exchanged rings, the traditional I do's, and we were married.

I flexed my hand, the thick platinum band heavy and warm on my skin. It looked so right there. It was simple, with a row of diamonds in the center and squared-off edges—modern-looking and sleek. Addi's engagement ring glinted in the light as she signed the paperwork, the diamond now joined by a matching band, marking her as taken. As mine.

The minister finished signing and handed me the paperwork, which I tucked into my pocket.

"It's official, Addi." I winked. "You can't get away now."

"Don't think I can run in these heels anyway."

I bent low and kissed her. "Good thing. I'd catch you anyway."

She drifted her fingers down my cheek. "Maybe we can play that game later."

A throat clearing beside me reminded me we weren't alone. I kissed her again. "You're on."

We followed the minister to the center of the arbor. My smile couldn't be contained as he lifted his voice.

"Ladies and gentlemen, I present to you, Mr. and Mrs. Brayden and Addison Riley."

The catcalls and clapping were loud as we made our way down the aisle.

We had done it. Addi was mine forever.

The weather cooperated, and outside was cold but not frigid. I had removed my tux jacket and donned my heavy cable-knit sweater and tugged my pea coat over it. I switched out my dress shoes for some warm boots. I made sure Lucy, the photographer, had extra blankets on hand, and I knew one of the photo sites had a fire pit going.

I watched Addi walk toward me, still beautiful, but also adorable at the same time. Her sweater was buttoned up, and she had a pair of matching mitts on her hands. A warm scarf topped her sweater, and when she held up her skirt, I grinned at the cute ankle boots trimmed in faux fur on her feet.

I greeted her with a kiss, keeping her cool lips underneath mine until they warmed up. Then the fun began. Lucy was all business, and for the next while, we posed with the backdrop of the snow and trees around us. Addi was a trooper, even sitting in the snow for a few shots while I stood over her, resting against a fallen log. Even with the benefit of the blanket under her, I felt her shiver and called for a moment. I took her to the fire, standing behind her and tucking her into my coat. She nestled against me, and I bent low, kissing her ear.

"Almost done. Then a couple of family shots, and we go inside."

She peeked up at me, her cheeks and the end of her nose pink from the cold. "I'm fine. This is fun!"

I had no choice but to kiss her again.

One of the assistants came over with steaming mugs of hot chocolate and some cupcakes. Addi grinned in delight, and I laughed as she bit into one, icing smearing on her nose. I kissed it off and let her feed me a bite, knowing the entire exchange was being captured on film. I had a feeling it would be one of my favorite pictures.

I took the wrapper from her, tossing it into the bin, just as a snowball hit me square in the back. I turned around, lifting one eyebrow.

"Really, Mrs. Riley?"

She grinned, her expression teasing and joyful. She tossed another snowball up in the air, catching it in her mitt.

"You dare me, Mr. Riley?"

It was on. Regardless of the fact that she was in a wedding dress and I was wearing a tux. We frolicked and threw snowballs, laughing and trash-talking. I made sure the only one that hit her landed on her arm, but my Addi was competitive and got me a few times in the chest. Then in a move I didn't expect, she lowered her shoulders, gathered her skirt, and tackled me. I fell back, luckily more on the blanket than the snow, and rolled her under me, kissing her with abandon. I loved seeing the free spirit come out in her. Sharing her joy of the day. Few saw this side of Addi, and it was one of my favorites.

We kissed, the world around us melting away. Her lips were cold, but her mouth warm as my tongue stole inside, licking and tasting her. Sweet icing, a hint of mint and chocolate, and all Addi. Groaning, I kissed her harder until a throat cleared.

"We should really wrap this up."

I gazed down at my bride. Her blue eyes were filled with mirth, dancing in the waning light.

"Look what you've done, Addi," I whispered, flexing my hips subtly. "A hard-on outside, with a photographer watching."

She grinned, wicked and happy. "I will remember this moment the rest of my life. Every time I see these pictures, I'll know."

I kissed her one more time. Hard and fast. "Little minx."

I stood, pulling her to her feet and brushing the snow off her dress. "You'll be cold and shivering the rest of the day." I fussed over her, the worry helping soften my erection.

"You'll keep me warm."

"Addi," I warned.

She shook her head. "The tulle will dry fast. And I'm wearing thermal leggings under here that I'll take off. We're all good."

"Time for the family shots," Lucy called. "They'll be here in a moment."

I was grateful as her assistant ran over, straightening the headpiece and fluffing Addi's hair. Luckily, her lipstick was kiss-proof, although I could see her lips were swollen from mine. I patted my hair into place and brushed off my pants. God forbid Bentley see us and figure out we were up to more than just some staged photos. I hadn't been his son-in-law long enough for him to be quite that forgiving that I was ravishing his daughter outside in the snow on our wedding day.

I'd save that for New Year's.

Hearing the sound of voices and laughter, I turned to greet our family.

While we were gone and our guests sipped various wines and champagnes offered here at the winery and indulged in decadent hors d'oeuvres, the hall was rearranged into a dining area with a huge dance floor. Candles flickered everywhere. The tables were covered in gold and ivory, with evergreens piled in the center and hurricane lamps glowing. Darkness was falling outside, and the trees and garland twinkled with white lights.

"It's so magical," Addi breathed beside me, her hand tightening on my arm.

"Is it what you wanted, Addi?"

She rose up on her toes and kissed my cheek. "The whole day has been perfect. More than I ever dreamed of." She pressed another kiss close to my lips. "Especially my groom."

"Then let's join our guests. We need to be sociable for the next few hours, then the fun really begins." I winked.

"Oh, you have a new board game you want to play?" she asked, blinking her eyes innocently. We loved playing board games—it helped us both to relax—and I liked finding older ones and learning to play them.

I grinned. "Oh, I'm going to play something, little elf. I plan on playing it all night long."

Her breath caught, and that delicious pink color surged under her skin, highlighting her cheeks.

"Well then, Mr. Riley, we'd best get at it."

"Excellent answer, Mrs. Riley."

ADDISON

I loved hearing Brayden call me Mrs. Riley. We had agreed, for business purposes, I would remain

Addison Ridge, but in my personal life, I would be Addison Riley.

I had been half in love with him my entire life. He was always there, a constant friend and supporter. I tried to date, feeling as if I shouldn't have the feelings I had for Brayden since we were almost family. But the few boys I had dated never measured up. I didn't feel the same way when they held my hand as I did when Brayden would. They looked bored when I would talk, as if they really didn't care what I had to say. Brayden always listened. Asked questions. Argued with me on subjects we didn't agree on. He challenged me. The bottom line was, he completed me. We fit as if made for each other. Once I got over my worry about our family ties, I accepted that—and him—entirely, and I had never looked back. Neither had he. Our course in life was tied with the other, and we were both happy to go with it.

I couldn't help my smile as they announced us, and we walked into the reception amid the loud applause. It wasn't a huge wedding by society standards. My dad and his partners kept their business and private life separate, so there were few unknown faces—mostly the plus-ones. Our social circle, and that of our parents, was tight-knit, so the numbers weren't large—our family made up most of the crowd.

Brayden swept me into his arms, and we danced our first dance as a couple, alone on the floor. He was an excellent dancer, and we moved well together. He held me tight in his arms, resting his head along mine and humming with the music, occasionally making quiet remarks.

"Our first dance of forever."

"You look beautiful in the candlelight, Addi."

"I love how you feel in my arms."

"Have I mentioned how much I love this dress?" He slid his hand up my spine, his long fingers splayed wide. "I'm looking forward to seeing how it looks on the floor of our bedroom later."

He pressed a kiss to my head. "And seeing what surprises you have on underneath it."

He dropped his head to my shoulder, running his mouth over my bare skin with light brushes of his lips. "Making love to my wife. Fucking her until she screams my name," he whispered darkly into my ear.

I felt flushed and breathless by the time we took our seats for dinner.

Brayden seemed calm, smiling and laughing, but I saw the desire in his eyes. Felt it in the grip he had on my hand. The way he kept me close, finding excuses to touch me. Throwing himself enthusiastically into the crowd's demands for kisses during dinner. The glasses would barely start clinking and he would be on his feet, dragging me into his arms, his mouth hard and possessive on mine.

Brayden had been my first and only lover. I was his. When we started dating, we had a frank discussion, and I told him I had always envisioned waiting for my wedding night. My virginity meant something to me, and unlike many girls at school, it wasn't something I was anxious to get rid of or give away.

The shocked look on his face would have made me laugh except for the seriousness of our talk. He was quiet for a moment, then took my hand.

"If that's what you want, Addi, I'll wait. We have the rest of our lives."

The next five years were filled with temptations. We kissed and touched, explored, learned the pleasure we could give each other, the pleasure we could take, without ever having actual intercourse. Orgasms were plentiful and enjoyable. I knew his body as well as he knew mine. We learned it all together, and although I knew there were times that Brayden wanted more, that his frustration levels had reached a maximum, he never lost his temper or pushed. He respected my decision, and although sometimes I was strongly tempted, I remained steadfast in my decision.

Until the night of Brayden's twenty-first birthday.

All he wanted was dinner with some friends, then to head to Port Albany. It was his favorite place on earth. We were surprised to find ourselves alone. Aiden was away with my dad and Maddox, looking at a piece of land up north. My mom was in Toronto, and although Cami had waved as we drove in, she didn't come to the house. We wandered to the beach, the night warm, the breeze light. We sat on a blanket, my back to Brayden's chest, looking at the stars as the night deepened and the silence surrounded us. I fingered the watch I had given him, the heavy silver links cool under my touch.

He pressed a kiss to my head. "I love it, Addi." He paused. "I love you."

I lifted my head, offering him my mouth. "I love you."

Our kiss started the way it always did. Soft and gentle. Then it changed, becoming deeper, longer. Taking and giving to each other, our tongues sliding and exploring. With a low groan, Brayden gathered me close, and seconds later, I was under him on the blanket. I loved how he felt on top of me. Solid, warm, and present. How his hands felt as they slid under my skirt, pushing up the fabric and teasing my skin. I whimpered as he ran his fingers over my center, the ache between my legs deeper and heavier than ever. All night, I had been watching him. He seemed different. Taller, his shoulders broad in the close-fitting shirt he wore, his muscular arms evident in the tight sleeves. We'd been so busy with school, work, and life, we hadn't been alone for a few weeks, and I had missed him. The desire I felt for him was overwhelming, and suddenly I knew.

"Make me yours," I whispered.

He drew back, surprise on his handsome face. "But Addi, you wanted to wait for your wedding night."

"I changed my mind." I slid my hand through his hair, cupping the back of his neck. "It's going to be you either tonight or then, right?"

"Absolutely."

I already wore a promise ring on my hand, and I knew he planned on changing it to an engagement ring soon.

"I don't want to wait anymore, Brayden. I want to be yours—in every way."

His green gaze was intense. I knew he was having an

inner argument—wanting to give me what I said I wanted, yet worried I would regret it.

Except I wouldn't. This was us—and we were forever.

"Make love to me."

"Here?"

I smiled. "This is our place. We're alone. I want you. Yes, here."

He crashed his mouth to mine and kissed me. Lifted me into his arms and carried me to his room. The house was silent as he set me on my feet.

"Are you sure?" he asked one last time.

I answered by tugging on the bows that held up my sundress. I rolled my shoulders, letting it fall to the floor, and I stood in front of him, my breathing hard. "Yes."

I smiled as I thought about our first time.

It wasn't perfect by any means. Our hands shook and searched, there were times our mouths were overeager, and our teeth clashed. He fell off the bed reaching into his nightstand for a condom. "Thank God Aiden gave me these as a joke last year," he mumbled. "I never thought I would need them, but I tossed them in here."

I giggled too hard when he struggled to rip it open, mumbling how much easier it looked in movies. We rolled and fumbled. Laughed, groaned, and apologized.

"I don't want to hurt you," he confessed. "I know the first time will."

"I'll be fine. I have you," I assured him. When he was finally seated inside me, he gazed down, his eyes burning in passion.

"Nothing prepared me for this," he hissed. "Jesus, Addi

—" He hung his head. "I'm not gonna last. You feel too good."

I was reeling from the way he felt. Filled by him and needing something. Something only he could give me. "Move, Brayden. Please move."

It was fast, intense, messy, and perfect. It was us.

And Brayden, it turned out, was a quick learner. He grew to be an amazing lover and, to this day, could turn me on with a look or a smile.

I expected very little sleep over the next couple of days.

And I was fine with that.

Another round of clapping brought me out of my memory-gathering. Brayden was standing, his hand held out, waiting for another kiss.

I was happy to accommodate. He grinned as he pulled me close. "What were you thinking about?" he asked quietly, gazing down at me. "Your cheeks are flushed again."

"Our first time," I whispered. "How amazing you felt inside me."

With a low growl, he kissed me. "Jesus, *wife*, you are killing me." He pulled me in tight, letting me feel his growing erection. "You keep doing this."

I grinned at the word "*wife*." I liked it. "I'll take care of that later, I promise."

Those words got me another deep kiss.

"I promise to take really good care of *you* tonight." He kissed me quickly. "Tomorrow." Another longer kiss followed. He bent me low, making me gasp and grip his shoulders. "The rest of our lives." Then he kissed me so long and hard, I forgot where I was.

It was perfect.

ꝏ

We had agreed to keep speeches short. Our parents kept theirs brief, my father far too emotional to say much, letting my mother speak. As the best man, Reed stood, approaching the microphone. Knowing his distaste for anything to do with public speaking, I knew it would be fast.

Except, he grinned into the microphone and looked over at us. "Sorry, friends. He's bigger and stronger. And he gave me a hundred bucks."

I watched as Aiden stood and approached the mic, pulling it from the stand. Both my father and Maddox dropped their heads, already grumbling, and Reid started laughing before Aiden began to speak.

Brayden groaned. "It's a wedding, Aiden. Not a roast."

"Have some faith, kid."

He turned to the mic. "For those of you who don't know me, I'm Aiden Callaghan. Adopted uncle, best friend, and all-around favorite boss of tonight's couple."

There was much laughter and taunts, which made Aiden smile.

"I've known these two kids since they were born. Before that, even. Twinkles in their fathers' eyes. The reason business suffered so greatly for a time because they were too busy with their own erections than the ones that the company was trying to build."

Everyone groaned. My dad dropped his head to the table in mock disgust. Maddox laughed, slapping him on the back. "Reed, Bent will give you five hundred to take back over," he called out.

Aiden pointed his finger at Reed. "Keep your ass in that chair, young man. I'll give you a grand to stay there."

Reed held up his hands. "I like where this is going."

I heard my dad groan. "I don't."

I chuckled. This was all too funny.

Aiden held his hand over his heart. "Imagine. My two best friends' kids getting married. Who would have dreamed that, all those years ago when we were poor university boys just trying to get by? Living hand to mouth, or in Bentley's case, million to million. Poor guy. We felt sorry for him, which is why we took him in. He was floundering, dripping money out of his pockets with nowhere to go."

That made my dad laugh.

"We're here today to celebrate something truly magical. Something so rare and fortuitous, it *has* to be celebrated. I am, of course, talking about the open bar. Holy shit, Bent. Did you know how much these people would drink? Good thing the groom's dad has access to the accounts—you're going to need it."

There was more laughter.

Aiden made some other jokes about us as kids but stuck to his word about keeping it brief and not going overboard.

Until the end.

"Marriage between the right two people is an amazing thing. It completes you in a way nothing else can." He looked over at us. "I wish you as much sex as I have had in my own marriage." He paused, scratching his head. "Wait. I mean success. I wish you a successful marriage."

He snorted with laughter at his own joke, while shaking his head at the whooping from the tables. "You guys are sick. I meant success."

"Sure, Dad!" one of the boys hollered.

Aiden winked. "I just want to add—may your ups and downs only be in the bedroom."

After the groans settled down, he became serious. "Stand with me and join in a toast. To two young people meant to be together. Their love is strong and beautiful. I'm proud to be their uncle, and I can hardly wait to see what the future brings for them. Or see Bentley bounce their child on his knee and be able to call him Gramps and get away with it." He lifted his glass. "To Brayden and Addi—the couple of the day."

He engulfed us both in his massive arms, lifting me right off the ground. "I did good, right?"

I chuckled. "Sure, Aiden." I pressed a kiss to his cheek. "You did real good."

Hours later, I smiled, remembering how proud he was of himself, as I sat down in a dark corner, the unexpected moment of quiet welcome. I had danced with my husband, my father, my new father-in-law, my brother, and Aiden. One turn with Aiden and I wasn't sure my body would recover. His strength and size didn't make for a good partner. And during the faster numbers, we all knew to give him a wide berth. His enthusiasm knew no bounds and made up for his lack of coordination. Cami usually just "held on for dear life," she told me once.

Pops, Reid, Van, Halton, Richard. My "cousins" insisted on their turns, and Ronan, Paul, Jeremy, Liam, Reed, Gavin, Theo, Matthew, and all the rest had claimed a dance. I bent low, rubbing my aching feet. I was grateful for the reprieve, although I didn't expect it to last long. Brayden would find me once he finished dancing with his mom and would want to dance some more. He loved to dance with me. In fact, he loved to dance period and moved with an easy grace. I was grateful for that.

Brayden's mom, Dee, looked lovely today, her mossy green dress complementing her soft red hair nicely. She smiled up at Brayden, their conversation constant since they'd started to dance. He was smiling indulgently down at her, towering over her as he did me. She had a couple of inches on me, but Brayden was six three, so he dwarfed both of us. He adored his mom, and she him. I was thrilled to have her as a mother-in-law. Like my own mom, she had been supportive of us from the beginning, saying it was destined to be.

It had been a great night, but I was grateful it was starting to wind down. Some guests had departed, and the ones who remained were mostly family. I liked it best that way. Brayden and I were in no hurry to leave since it was our wedding and party, and we were enjoying ourselves. But I knew soon he would come take my hand, and we would leave the last of the partiers to shut the place down.

I had a feeling the night would end with my father, Aiden, Maddox, Reid, Van, Halton, and Richard sitting at the last table, feet kicked up, a bottle of whiskey between them, lamenting how their kids had grown up too fast. They'd trade stories and heartbreaks, trying to outdo one another. For such stern businessmen, they were a bunch of softies when it came to their families. I loved them all for it.

I leaned back my head, the sound of a hushed conversation behind me making me perk up my ears. I recognized Gracie's voice. Her plus-one had been unexpected and mysterious. She had introduced me to him as he came through the receiving line. Her lips had been tight as she spoke.

"Brayden, Addi, this is Jaxson Richards, my, ah, coworker. He helped get me here."

Jaxson's eyebrows lifted at the introduction, but he didn't say anything. We thanked him, and he shook Brayden's hand, congratulating us on our nuptials, then lifted my hand and kissed it. "A pleasure."

I noticed a few things about him immediately. He was drop-dead gorgeous. His hair was so dark, it was almost black. He was tall, broad, and his suit was custom tailored. His jaw was chiseled, with a deep cleft in the middle. He carried himself easily, his confidence evident. He looked stern and haughty—serious, without humor. His eyes were a startling blue, piercing and shrewd.

And they were focused intently on my best friend, whereas she was trying to look everywhere but at him. Her over-the-top casualness made it obvious that whoever he was, whatever he was to her, it was not casual.

And the third thing was the fact that around his ring finger was the same pinched pink line I'd noticed on Gracie's hand earlier.

I could tell I was the only one who noticed. Brayden was already greeting the next guest, and everyone else was too busy enjoying themselves.

Jaxson lingered in front of Gracie, speaking in a low tone, then moved on, heading to the bar. He took a glass of champagne and headed toward the table where Katy was sitting. Beside me, Gracie tensed.

"Did you put him with my parents?" she asked, horrified.

"I don't honestly know. Jen arranged a spot for him. Is that a problem?" I asked.

"Um, no, of course not. It's just he and Dad will probably talk business all night."

I lifted my eyebrows so she knew I knew how full of BS she was. Then I turned to greet the next guest. We would continue this conversation later.

Even though Jaxson had only spoken a few words to me earlier, I recognized his deep tenor.

"Why should I leave, Gracie? I'm enjoying myself."

"Stop calling me that. It's Grace."

"All your family calls you Gracie."

"You aren't my family."

"Hmm. I beg to differ."

I sat up straighter. *What?*

"You shouldn't be here," Gracie insisted.

"You're here. I belong at your side."

"No, you don't," she hissed.

"I imagine the law would agree with me."

"Fuck the law," she almost growled, shocking me. Grace rarely swore. She rarely got upset. It was one of the reasons she was going to be such a good lawyer.

The next words I heard shocked me even more.

"I would rather fuck *you* again, darling. Far more enjoyable."

There was an odd choking noise, and then I heard the sound of footsteps hurrying away. High-heeled ones. Then a low chuckle and that deep voice murmuring a quiet promise.

"Run, Gracie, my darling. I'll catch you, regardless."

Jaxson Richards stepped out from behind the corner. He noticed me and lifted his eyebrows with a smirk. He bent close. "Your boss is funny."

"He's not just my boss."

He smiled suddenly, changing his face. It went from haughty to open. His dimple deepened as he grinned, and his eyes danced. He was devastatingly handsome. He tilted his chin toward the direction he and Gracie had been standing. "I'm not just her boss either."

Then he headed toward the table he'd been sitting at, leaving me gaping at his retreating back. He didn't appear upset or worried. If anything, his confidence was higher.

I slipped around the corner and into the ladies' room that was at the end of the hall. It was deserted except for Grace. She stood, gripping the counter, her head down, and her shoulders taut.

I stepped behind her.

"Gracie."

She whirled around, her eyes wide and startled.

"What is going on?" I asked quietly. "Don't tell me nothing because we both know that's a lie."

She sighed. "Remember me telling you about the pompous jackass I work for?"

I nodded. "It's Jaxson?" I guessed. "He's not just a coworker, but your boss. Your *direct* boss."

"Yes. He specializes in corporate law. I'm his intern. The firm sent us both to Vegas to work on this copyright mess we've been dealing with."

"Is he any good?"

"He's brilliant," she admitted. "When we're in the zone, we work really well together. The problem is we strike sparks the rest of the time. We're constantly battling with each other."

I waited. There was more to the story, but she wasn't telling me everything.

"When I missed my plane, and the snowstorm hit, he helped me get here. I never would have made it if it weren't for him. Part of the deal was he got to come to the wedding."

"Okay?"

She waved her hand. "I told him it was enough. To go home. He's been here far too long already. He refuses to leave."

"Why?"

She pressed her lips together. "Can we drop it?"

"No. Why is he refusing to leave, Gracie? Why were you so upset that he was sitting at your parents' table?"

"I don't want him getting comfortable with them."

"Why? If he's your boss and he helped you, what's the big deal?"

She began to turn away, but I refused to allow it. I grabbed her arm. "What happened in Vegas, Gracie?"

She met my eyes. "I married him."

CHAPTER 5
ADDISON

Before I could recover from the bombshell Gracie had just dropped, the washroom door opened, and Heather, Gracie's sister, came in.

"There you are. Nan and Pops are leaving, Bray is looking for you, Addi, and Gracie, that sexy coworker of yours is prowling around like a dementor. Does he suck the happiness out of every room he enters?"

She finished off her rapid announcement with a hand on her hip, looking exasperated. "He's a bossy SOB, isn't he?"

Gracie blinked, then let out an uncharacteristic giggle. My lips quirked at Heather's tone. The two sisters physically looked alike. Both small with dark hair and delicate features like their mom, Katy, but while Gracie had blue eyes like their mom, Heather had Richard's hazel eyes that seemed to see everything. That was where the resemblance ended.

Gracie was calm, quiet, and unflappable, while Heather was exuberant, creative, and loud. She spoke her mind and used her hands to make a point, as if she were painting a picture for you. Despite their differences, they had always been close, but Gracie had obviously not shared her news with her sister.

"He is a bit over the top," Gracie stated, smoothing her hands down the front of her dress. "I imagine he's leaving and wanted to say his farewells."

Heather shook her head. "I don't think so. He told Mom he's alone at Christmas since he has no family, and she invited him to stay. She offered him the spare room."

Gracie paled. "What? He doesn't need the spare room. He has his own home in Toronto."

Heather glanced in the mirror, tucking a loose tendril behind her ear. "He told her that."

Gracie blew out a relieved breath. "Oh. Okay."

Heather grinned. "He said he'd love to come back, though, so he'll be here Christmas morning." She grabbed the door handle. "I guess Christmas just took on a different feel. I hope he learns to smile by then. Come say goodbye to Nan and Pops."

She left in traditional Heather style, a whirlwind of fabric and her signature lilac scent.

Gracie and I exchanged glances. "Well." I smirked. "This is gonna be interesting."

She grabbed my hand. "You can't say anything, Addi. It was a mistake, and it will be corrected. It's private." Her eyes widened. "My dad cannot find out. He'll go berserk."

"I won't say anything, but I want the whole story."

"I'll tell you," she promised. "Just let me get through this mess first. I need to go and uninvite Mr. Richards."

I couldn't help it. "Gracie?"

"What?"

"If you stayed married to him and hyphenated your name, maybe you could use Grace Richards-VanRyan. Sort of a twist, you know? Your dad might actually like that." I tried to hold in my laughter, but a chuckle escaped my lips.

For a moment, her lips quirked, then she frowned. "Addi, that was uncalled-for. I think you're channeling your inner Aiden." She yanked open the door. "And this marriage is history. It never happened," she hissed quietly.

Still chuckling, I followed her slowly, thinking about Jaxson's remark and the determined look on his face.

I had a feeling Mr. Richards might not agree.

BRAYDEN

Gracie rushed past me, heading toward the table where her mother sat with the guy she'd brought as her plus-one. Jason? Justin? I couldn't remember. He seemed pretty intense, but I had other things on my mind right now.

Specifically, finding my bride.

She appeared ahead of me, and I strode toward her. "I've been looking for you, Mrs. Riley."

She grinned. "Are you ever going to get tired of calling me that?"

I bent and kissed her. "I have waited a long time to be able to call you that, so nope. I will never tire of it. Pops and Nan are leaving, and I think I've partied enough."

She grimaced. "I won't argue there. My feet are aching from all the dancing. And I'm hungry."

"If you'd eat something, you wouldn't be so hungry. You've only picked all night."

"I can barely breathe in this corset thing, let alone eat," she admitted. "I want out of it."

"That's a plan I can get behind. Go say good night to Pops and Nan. I'll get you a snack."

She rose up and kissed me, her lips warm and soft. "Thank you."

"Anytime."

She floated away, her skirts billowing around her. I headed to the kitchen and ten minutes later found her still talking to Nan. Pops stood to the side,

Nan's coat draped over his arm as he listened to their conversation, a bemused smile on his face.

Sandy looked incredible. Her pure-white hair was swept up and away from her face, the vivid blue of her dress lovely with her coloring. She had lots of laugh lines around her eyes and mouth but refused to worry about them. *"I've earned them," she liked to say.*

Still, her eyes were bright and her smile wide. She walked with a slight limp since her hip replacement, but she was active and energetic. Aiden made sure of that. Jordan was tall and strong, always close in case she needed him. They were a great couple and the best grandparents around. We were all lucky to have them as part of our lives.

Nan saw me approach and beamed. "There he is. You ready to take your bride away from all this?"

I kissed her cheek. "Her feet hurt and she's hungry." I indicated the basket I was holding. "I had the kitchen pack up some tidbits for us."

"Already a good husband." She patted my cheek. "Just like your father."

My dad doted on my mother. She was devoted to him as well. It was a good example to try to follow.

I glanced around, noting Gracie in a serious conversation with her plus-one. He was listening to her, leaning on a pillar, sipping a brandy with a small smirk on his face. She looked pretty hot and bothered, but he seemed at ease and not at all put out by her gestures or the words she was flinging at him. Cami, Emmy, Mom, Katy, Liv, Fee, and Becca were at a table together, watching them. Heather was dancing with Reed, the two of them wrapped around each other as per usual.

"Where are the guys?"

Jordan snorted as he slipped Sandy's coat over her shoulders. "On the balcony with a bottle of scotch. I think Bentley is wallowing, and his boys are with him for moral support."

Addi's gaze drifted to the glass doors. "Daddy," she murmured, looking sad.

Sandy chuckled. "He's fine. Let him have his pout with his band of misfits. It'll be their turn soon enough." She indicated Grace and Heather. "I think Richard needs to prepare himself."

"I think he's accepted Reed. He likes him."

"It took a while, though."

"True." Richard had thought Reed and Heather were only friends. Until the time he flew in unexpectedly and caught them kissing in the office. That had been an interesting day.

Reed and Heather were still a fairly new item. When she arrived in Toronto, he had been friendly and offered to show her around. None of us thought anything about it, until they started arriving at the office together, holding hands. I knew Bentley had spoken to them, reminding them of the policies in the office.

"You break up? You keep it between you. I have zero problem getting rid of trouble. You understand?"

They only seemed to grow closer. They kept their PDA behind closed doors for the most part. Although their teasing and quips often made me chuckle during meetings.

I was talking to my dad in the hall when a familiar voice rang out.

"Mad Dog!"

We turned to see Richard striding down the hall.

He and my dad shook hands and gave each other a one-armed hug. "What are you doing here?"

"Heather sounded strange on the phone. I was a bit worried, so I decided to come see for myself what was going on."

My dad and I exchanged a glance. I hadn't noticed anything off with Heather. "She seems fine to me," I offered. "But I'm sure she'll be thrilled to see you. She's in her office," I added.

"I'll go surprise her."

He disappeared around the corner, and I heard a knock, then silence, followed by another knock. Heather only ever closed her door if she needed privacy.

I frowned and looked at my dad, panicked. "If Heather's door is closed…" I let my voice trail off. "Does he know about Reed?"

"What the hell?" Richard bellowed.

"I think he does now." My dad smirked.

We raced around the corner. Richard was standing in front of Heather's desk. Reed and Heather were behind it, both looking rumpled. Heather's mouth was swollen, and Reed's hair was messy, as if someone's fingers had been in it. Namely, Heather's.

"You had better tell me that Heather was choking and you were providing assistance," Richard snarled.

"Daddy," Heather protested. "Don't be ridiculous."

"Don't you 'Daddy' me," Richard demanded. "What is going on?"

Reed straightened his shoulders. "I was kissing Heather." He put his hand on her shoulder. "My girlfriend."

Richard inhaled sharply. "Your girlfriend?"

Heather slid her hand over Reed's. "His girlfriend," she repeated.

Richard looked at my dad. "Did you know?"

"Recently, yes. I thought she had told you." My dad pulled on my arm. "We'll leave you to, ah, talk." He paused. "And Richard?"

"What?"

"No blood. We don't allow blood during business hours."

"I can't promise anything."

"Dad! Stop overreacting!"

"I'll decide when I'm overreacting, young lady."

She rolled her eyes. "Give me strength. I'm calling Mom."

"She'll be on my side on this one."

Heather picked up the phone. "We'll see."

My dad and I backed out of the office, pulling the door shut.

"Is that a good idea?"

He grinned. "If you survived Bentley, Reed can handle Richard. He's been working out with Aiden and Van. He can take him."

"You're really not worried?"

"I have no doubt Heather will calm him down. Especially if Katy is involved." He clapped my shoulder. "I am getting too old for this shit."

Richard had calmed down eventually. He had always liked Reed, so that helped. His trips to visit happened more frequently for a while, though.

Nan's throat-clearing brought me back to the present. "And Jaxson?" she asked, her eyebrow raised.

"Ah, that's just Gracie's boss," Addi replied, looking uncomfortable. "He helped her get here today."

Sandy leaned forward and kissed her. "And Richard was Katy's boss. History has a way of repeating itself."

They left, and I slid my arm around Addi. "Ready?"

"I think so."

Bentley suddenly appeared in front of us. He smelled of cigar smoke and scotch, and his normally shrewd gaze was cloudy. He cupped Addi's cheek. "Be happy, baby girl. Don't forget me."

She struggled to hold back her grin. "I'll see you in two days, Dad."

"I know. Cut me a little slack, okay? I love you."

"I love you too. Now go back to the balcony and finish your cigar. No more scotch."

He chuckled and reached out for my hand,

shaking it wildly. "Welcome to the family, Brayden. I'm happy you're my son-in-law."

"Thanks, Bent."

"Hurt her, and I will dissect you into such small pieces, they'll never find you."

I blinked. "Good to know."

Then he grinned. "Nah. Kidding."

He walked away, calling over his shoulder. "Aiden will, though."

He stopped by the table and bent to kiss Emmy. She said something to him, and he waved his hand. He headed back to the balcony, and all the women at the table burst into laughter.

I chuckled. "I think your dad is a bit drunk. I've never seen him drunk."

"It's been a hard day for him."

I bent close and kissed her. "You okay?"

She sighed and leaned her head on my shoulder. "Yeah, but I can't take much more emotion tonight. Can we slip out, or is that rude?"

I looked over to the mothers' table and indicated the door with my chin. Emmy and my mom nodded and waved, both still looking amused.

I kissed Addi's head. "We're covered. The car is out front. Let's go."

She picked up her purse and the cardigan. "I'm with you."

"I can walk!" Addi protested as I slipped her from the car and into my arms.

"Nope. I'm carrying you over the threshold. It's tradition."

"Oh." She relaxed in my arms. "Okay, then."

I chuckled, dropping a kiss to her head. "Besides, you fell asleep before we even left the parking lot. You're exhausted, my little elf."

Inside, I set her on the sofa. "Stay." I waggled my finger.

She rolled her eyes dramatically. "So it begins."

Laughing, I returned to the car and grabbed the basket, returning to the warmth of the house. I set down the basket and held out my hand. "Let's get you out of that dress so you can eat."

She sighed. "I imagined you peeling it off me in the bedroom and ravishing me right after."

"How about I peel it off you, kiss every inch I uncover, then we can eat and relax." I smiled at her indulgently. "We have the rest of the night for me to ravish you." I chuckled at her trying to cover up her yawn, and I held out my hand. "Come with me."

In our bedroom, she gasped. I'd had it filled with flowers and candles while we were gone, wanting it romantic for her. There was a bottle of champagne chilling and a single rose on her pillow.

"Bray." She turned to me, her hands clasped. "It's so beautiful."

I bent and kissed her, pulling her close. Our lips moved effortlessly, soft and sweet. I pulled back, spinning her, and got to work on the buttons that had mocked me all day. One by one, I slid them open, tracing her spine with my lips. The small zipper at the bottom slid down easily, and in an instant, the dress was a pile of froth and glitter on the floor. I traced the indents of the stays that remained on her sides, hating the fact that they had marred her skin and amazed she had walked around all day smiling while they had pinched at her flesh.

She turned with a smile. "They don't hurt." I held out my hand, and she stepped from the material. I bent down, unbuckling the strappy shoes and sliding them off her feet. I kissed each instep, rubbing them. I looked up at her.

"You were so beautiful today for me, Addi. Breathtaking."

Color flushed her cheeks. I slid my hands up her calves, the silky skin smooth under my fingers. I stood slowly, letting my fingers trail over her body as I drew to my full height. "But I think you are the most beautiful when you're just Addi. Alone with me, without the corset or the makeup. I see the real you. The most beautiful woman in the world because you are that way inside and out."

Tears filled her eyes. I cupped her cheeks. "I'm the luckiest man in the world because I have you. Now I want you to wash your face, put on one of my shirts, and come to the living room. I want to sit by the fire and feed you. Hold you. That's all I want right now. Let me do that."

She covered my wrists with her fingers, squeezing them. "How did I get so lucky?"

I nudged her nose with mine. "I guess we both did."

Then I winked at her. "Now go, before my dick overrides my head and I ravish you first. My god, you are sexy." I traced the wisp of lace at her hips. "Keep these on. I want to take them off—with my teeth."

She sashayed away, winking at me over her shoulder.

"Whatever you want, Mr. Riley. I'm all yours."

It was all I could do not to follow her.

"Married?" I gasped. "Gracie is *married?* To that guy? Jerome?"

She giggled around a mouthful of a sandwich. The kitchen had packed up a veritable feast. We had sandwiches, cheeses, assorted pickles, and condiments from the midnight buffet. Plus cake and cookies. I had refused their offer of the filet of beef and other items, asking them to donate it all to a shelter as we had requested. What they gave us barely made a dent in the leftover food, and I was happy to know the rest would help feed those in need. I had filled a plate for us to share, and we had both tucked in.

"Jaxson," she corrected.

"Whatever. Gracie is *married?* Holy shit, Richard is going to blow a gasket."

"She doesn't want him to know. She says it was a mistake and it will be handled."

I snorted as I reached for another sandwich. I had hardly eaten earlier either, and now I was starving. "Katy invited him for Christmas. You know it's going to come out."

"I'm the only one who knows. Well, and you now. You can't say anything."

I shook my head in disbelief. "I can't believe, of all of us, Gracie would be the one to get drunk and marry someone in Vegas. Her intense, I-could-kill-you-with-my-bare-hands-looking boss, of all people. And she expects it to remain a secret. The way he was looking at her? Good luck with that."

"I think she was going to tell him he couldn't come."

I sat back and pursed my lips. "I don't think he is gonna listen. This is going to be one for the records."

Addi worried her lip. "This is so unlike her."

"No shit. It's something one of the triplets would do. Maybe even Shelby. But Gracie?" I let my head fall back. "Do you think she's in love with him?"

"All she has ever said was he was hard to work

for. I never even knew his name until today." Addi shrugged. "He is handsome, though. Sexy with that smolder."

I narrowed my eyes. "I beg your pardon? He's *what*?"

She laughed. "Not as handsome as you, of course. He's way too dark and broody for me. For Gracie too, I would have thought. But who knows?"

I huffed.

Addi picked up a slice of cake and nibbled it. She licked her lips, staring into the fire. I loved the way she looked right now. Dressed in one of my hoodies, her legs bare. Her face scrubbed clean of makeup and her hair down around her shoulders. I had changed as well, wearing only a pair of sweatpants and a loose Henley. Comfort was the key. Sitting across from each other on the blanket I had spread out, eating an indoor picnic, sipping champagne, and talking was exactly what we needed to do. Reliving the day and, of course, the bombshell Addi had dropped. It made no sense to me. Gracie —married. She was the most sensible of us all. Level-headed. She thought everything through. An impulsive marriage to a brooding, older man? Her boss, no less? I really wanted to hear that story.

But as I studied my wife, I wanted something else more.

Reaching across the blanket, I tugged her over, settling her between my legs. She leaned back into my chest with a soft sigh, drawing her legs up to her chest. I wrapped my arms around her, content to feel her close for the time being.

"For the next two days, you're mine, Addi. I'm locking the cell phones and laptops away. No one is coming near the house. I'm not sharing you until Christmas Day."

"I like the sound of that."

"I got a little tree we can put up tomorrow if you want. I even bought some decorations."

"I love that!"

"I figured there was no point in a big one since the Hub has the family tree. But I wanted you to have a little one this year. We'll pick a bigger one next year and put it up earlier."

Addi loved Christmas. We all did. The tradition had been the same since I was a small child. Each family had their own Christmas morning, then at lunch, we gathered together at the Hub. We exchanged gifts, went sledding or ice-skating, played outside. Ate cookies and drank hot cocoa. Everyone, right down to the youngest, pitched in for dinner. The women mostly handled the cooking, and the men the cleanup, although I recalled my dad often in the kitchen.

I remembered folding napkins, setting the table, crumbling bread for the stuffing. Years of memories were in that building. The hot cocoa became cider, the cups of milk at dinner replaced by wine, the board games after dinner replaced by movies. But it was the gathering of our families that remained constant.

There was always one gift under our tree at home from Santa and a stocking filled with goodies and little trinkets. My parents had explained that Santa could only leave one gift as he was too busy to do all the shopping, and they helped him with the rest. Family gifts were opened at home, and at the Hub were the ones from Pops and Nan, and the rest of the crew. Names were drawn months in advance. Otherwise, with the number of us, it would have gotten out of hand. But Nan and Pops insisted on buying everyone something.

When we were all really little, Santa came to see us on Christmas Day. His sack would be filled with candy, and we all got to sit on his knee. We never knew when he would show up, but he always did. His laughter was loud and familiar, and it was a long time before we caught on to the fact that it was Aiden under the beard and false belly. I think Gracie took it the hardest when Santa stopped visiting—even if she was older and knew the truth long before the rest of us did.

It was always a day filled with love and laughter, and more times than not, we drifted off, exhausted from the long day. We would fall asleep in the Hub and wake in our own beds the next morning. Even now, once dishes were done, lots of naps happened, especially by the men, sitting on the sofas, replete and tired from the constant craziness of the days leading up to Christmas, not to mention the day itself.

"Our first Christmas as husband and wife," Addi mused. "I feel as if we should have our own tradition."

I kissed the crown of her head. "How about each year, Christmas Eve is just us? Here in the house alone."

"I like that."

"Okay. This year will be the first."

We were silent for a moment, watching the fire, listening to the wind outside, wrapped in the warmth of each other.

"Are you sorry we didn't wait, Addi?" I asked quietly. We hadn't made love since December 1. In a stupid moment of remembrance, I had suggested it would build anticipation for tonight. I had regretted that impulsive idea until this very moment. The longing I felt for her couldn't be any deeper. My desire was so intense I could taste it in the air. Feel it pulsating under my skin.

Still, I wondered if she had any regrets.

She tilted her head back, meeting my eyes. "To make love?"

"Yes. I know you had wanted to wait for your first time to be your wedding night."

She smiled, stroking my jaw softly with her fingers. "It will be, Brayden. It will be our first time as husband and wife. It's still special, because it's us. It will only ever be us."

Her words filled my heart, and I lowered my head, kissing her. As soon as my mouth touched hers, heat filled me. I gathered her close, sliding my tongue into her mouth and kissing her with all the love and passion I felt for her.

Addi whimpered, wrapping her arms around my neck and pulling me in deeper. Endlessly we kissed. Long, hot kisses of passion. Soft, loving presses of our lips. Gentle nips and deep passes of our tongues as we explored. I ran my hands over her, groaning as I delved under the long hoodie to her bare skin. I fingered the lace on her hips, recalling the small band of silk between her legs. I kissed up and down her neck, laving my tongue on her skin, nibbling her ear, my breathing picking up, my cock hardening.

She gripped my hair, tugging on the short strands. Slid her hands up my back, tracing along my spine. Ran her nails along my skin, making me shudder. Straddled me, pressing her heat down onto my erection.

In one fluid movement, I stood, taking her with me, grateful for the lunges Aiden made me do. In our room, I set her on the bed, tugging the hoodie over her head. She leaned back on her arms, looking small and sexy against the deep gray of the comforter. In seconds, I was naked, and she shifted back into the middle of the bed. I leaned over her, hooking my fingers around the lace and silk that hid her from me. I was too impatient to use my teeth. I would save that for the next time.

"These have to go. *Now*."

They joined the pile of clothes on the floor, and I stared down at my wife. She was perfect. Tiny enough to fit under my arm but formed for me and me alone. Her high breasts with their rosy nipples that I loved to kiss and suck. Wide hips and a sweet indentation at her waist that I could span with my hands. Small feet with even smaller toes and nails that she kept covered in polish—changing the color constantly so I never knew what it would be. Surprisingly long legs for someone so short, and at the apex—the sweetest, tightest pussy in the world that was all mine. I loved being inside her. The clutch and pull of her muscles, the heat that encased me when we were joined so closely you couldn't see where I ended and she began.

"Brayden," she murmured, breaking me from my thoughts.

I crawled up the mattress, kissing her. Settling between her thighs, stroking her skin. Passion flared, and we moved together as the heat kicked in. We kissed and caressed. Tasted and licked. I nipped at her breasts, teasing the tight peaks. She rolled us over and did the same to me, kissing her way down my abdomen and taking me in her mouth. I arched off the bed as she sucked me, rolling my balls in her hand and taking me deep. I could only take it for a short time before I rolled us again and lapped at her. She cried out as I sucked her hard nub into my mouth and slid two fingers into her, pumping slowly, drawing out her pleasure. We feasted on each other until we were breathless, sweaty, and aching. Frantic. I flung her legs over my shoulders and slid into her. I shut my eyes at the feeling of her surrounding me. It felt like the first time, all over again.

"Welcome home, Mr. Riley," she murmured, cupping my face.

"God, I love you, Addison Riley," I replied, aching with the emotion of the moment. Aching for her.

"Please, Brayden," she begged, drawing me down to her mouth. "Please."

I kissed her, the taste of us on her lips. I began to move, holding her leg high, hitting her where she liked me the most. As deep as I could get inside her. She whimpered my name, clutching at my damp skin, moving with me. Like the waves outside, we flowed and ebbed. Rose and fell. Cresting together until she shook, her eyes going wide as her orgasm rushed through her and my name fell from her lips. I thrust once, twice more and succumbed to the mind-numbing pleasure I had only felt with her—would only ever feel with her—racing through me. I groaned her name, gathering her close, riding out the ecstasy.

Then slowly, carefully, I eased her back to the bed and slipped from her. I lay beside her, tucking her close.

She pressed a kiss to my damp skin. "I love you."

I held her tight. The love of my life. My precious wife.

"Always, Addi. Always and forever."

PART II

CHRISTMAS

CHAPTER 6
BRAYDEN

I woke up, my hand reaching for Addi and only finding an empty bed. It was still new and wonderful to wake up beside her, knowing it would happen for the rest of our life together. The weekends and occasional night she would stay here were never enough.

We had barely left the bedroom since we got married. Except when we grabbed something to eat or a shower, and even then, something would happen. Addi would wink or look at me *that* way, and instantly my dick was hard, and we'd end up on the floor, on top of the counter, by the fire, or against the cold tiles in the shower. We'd christened a lot of spots in the house, but luckily, we had many left to try.

I should be exhausted, but I'd never felt more alive.

Except my wife was missing. I peered at the

clock—it was barely six. She should be asleep beside me, tucked into a ball the way she always slept. Nestled close for warmth, hogging all the covers, her head on my pillow, and her warm breath on my skin.

Our bathroom door was open, but the door to the hall was pulled closed, and I knew I would find her by the tree, dressed in her elf pajamas, as excited as a five-year-old, and waiting for me. She always liked to get up early and sit in the darkness with only the lights of the tree in the room. She told me once she loved greeting Christmas morning that way. When we were dating, I would sneak over to her house and scale the balcony to sit with her, enjoying the peacefulness of the early morning with her before the frenzy began. When Bentley found me with her one Christmas morning, there was hell to pay, and from then on, I used the front door.

It was still dark when I snuck out of the house, pulling the door shut quietly behind me. I hiked across the snow-covered beach, the route familiar although more treacherous this time of the year. I scaled the balcony of Addi's family home and peeked in the window. My little elf was beside the huge tree, wrapped in a blanket, the glow of the lights reflecting on her face. I tapped lightly, and she looked up, waving me in. The door slid open without a squeak, and I left my shoes on the deck. I flung my coat over the sofa and headed toward her. She opened the blanket, and I slid in behind her, wrapping my arms around her and pulling her back to me. I dropped my face to her neck, kissing the skin. "You're so warm."

She shivered. "And you're freezing. I told you not to come, Brayden—it's too dangerous."

"It's fine. I want a little time with you today alone."

Although we'd been together for over two years, Bentley still preferred when we hung out as a group. We would be surrounded the rest of the day, with maybe a chance or two to sneak off for some stolen alone time, but it never lasted long. Someone, usually Bentley or Aiden, always found us. Ronan was good at it too, although he at least dragged his feet while searching. I never got to kiss her as much as I wanted on Christmas. I looked forward to the day I could.

I slipped a small box into her hand. "For you."

She lifted her head and offered me her mouth. "Thank you."

I kissed her softly, knowing we couldn't get carried away. She opened the box, gasping in delight at the promise ring inside. Delicate like her, it was a simple band of gold with tiny emeralds in it. She loved my eyes, and I wanted the ring to remind her of me.

"Wear it until the day I replace it with a diamond," I whispered, sliding it on her finger.

"I love it."

She took my wrist, snapping on an intricately woven leather and silver band. The medallion in the middle had our initials engraved, the A and B entwined. It was heavy and masculine.

I kissed her again. "It's perfect. You're perfect. I love you, Addi."

"I love you."

A light snapped on, startling us. "And I'd love to know what the hell you're doing in my house at five thirty in the morning, Brayden Riley. How the hell did you get in here?" Bentley's voice was dark and angry.

Both Addi and I scrambled to our feet, the blanket falling away.

"We aren't doing anything," I protested. "I just wanted to give Addi her gift."

"And that couldn't wait until the sun came up?" He narrowed his eyes. "Where the hell is your coat?" He stepped forward, anger turning to fury. "Have you been here all night?"

I held up my hands. "No! No, Uncle Bentley! I just got here, like, ten minutes ago. I just wanted a little time alone with her today. You know how much she loves Christmas. I got her something special, and I wanted to give it to her. I swear!" I knew I was rambling, but the look on his face was scary.

"How did you get in?"

"Over the balcony."

He looked over my shoulder. "You climbed over the balcony? Something wrong with the front door?"

"I knew Addi was in here, so it made more sense," I replied, my answer sounding more like a question.

"You knew she was in here," he repeated slowly. "You've done this before, I take it."

Shit. I shouldn't have said that.

Emmy appeared. "What is going on?"

"Young Brayden here decided to pay our daughter a little Christmas morning visit."

"How sweet." She smiled at me.

"It's not sweet," he snarled. "It's practically the middle of the night."

"You're overreacting, Rigid."

"Overreacting? He came over the balcony, Emmy. He's done it before."

"Oh." She looked at me with a slight frown, although her eyes were dancing. "Maybe you should use the front door next time."

Bentley dug his phone from his robe pocket, hitting a button. He waited a moment, then spoke.

"Mad Dog? Your son is in my house, having a little morning visit with my daughter. He came in via the balcony. I just thought you should know he's going out the same way. And he's heading home fast because I'm not giving him his shoes. Maybe he'll remember that next time."

He hung up, heading my direction. I had no choice. I grabbed Addi, kissing her. "Merry Christmas, little elf!"

I took off running, not bothering to try for my coat or shoes. I headed toward the steps, swinging myself over the railing when I got close enough to the bottom. I gasped at the cold of the icy ground, but I didn't stop. Behind me, Addi was yelling at her dad, and Emmy was giving him shit. I sprinted over the beach and used the shortcut to head to my parents' place. My nipples felt like shards of glass, and my dick was so cold, I swore it was trying to crawl up inside my body. My feet were numb, but I kept going. My dad was waiting for me, shaking his head as he opened the door.

"Brayden—"

I held up my hand. "I know. I'll apologize."

"You'll have to."

"We weren't doing anything—just exchanging gifts," I defended myself.

He chuckled. "He's gonna be hell on wheels for the next while, you know that."

"The way Addi and Emmy were yelling at him, he might not be as bad as you think." I shivered.

He pushed me toward the fire. "Warm yourself, and I'll make coffee. I don't think I'll be going back to sleep now."

I headed to the fire, the heat feeling good on my feet. The rest of my anatomy began to warm up as well. My phone buzzed in my pocket, and a message from Addi appeared.

Addi: ***I'm sorry.***

I replied.

Brayden: ***So worth it. I love you.***

Her response warmed my heart.

Addi: ***I love you too. Heather is going to cover this afternoon. I'll thank you properly in the library at two. Be there.***

I grinned as I felt the feeling come back to my feet.

Brayden: *Wouldn't miss it for the world.*

I chuckled remembering that day and Bentley's cool attitude that lasted about three hours. I apologized and promised only to use the front door and not show up before dawn. He brought my coat back but informed me since he couldn't toss me in the lake, he'd sacrificed my shoes instead.

"Consider yourself lucky," he informed me.

I took him at his word.

But it reminded me of needing to find my wife.

I sat up, and a Santa hat fell from my chest to my lap, the bright red and white vivid on the dark comforter. Laughing, I pulled it on my head and went to find my wife.

She was by the tree as I expected, the fireplace going, the lights bright in the early morning dimness. I slid behind her, pulling her back to my chest and wrapping my arms around her.

"Merry Christmas, Mrs. Riley."

She tilted up her head. "Merry Christmas, Mr. Riley."

Our lips met, moving gently. I pulled back, and she leaned into me. "I love this time of the day."

"I know."

"Our tree is so cute."

I chuckled. The little pine tree I had bought was only about two feet tall. We were barely able to get one small strand of lights and about half a dozen little ornaments on it before it looked as if it would collapse.

"We'll have a bigger one next year," I promised. "I thought we'd plant this one by the deck."

"I love that idea."

"Did you want to open your gifts?" I asked. We'd agreed to keep things simple this year, but we had each bought the other a few gifts, and they looked pretty with the bright wrapping under the tree. Addi's looked far nicer with her neat corners and perfectly centered bows, but I thought my slightly askew wrapping job was at least decent. She'd like what was inside for sure.

"Later."

She picked up a cup of coffee and sipped it, then offered it to me. I hummed in appreciation at the intense flavor. We both liked it strong and black, and this cup tasted even better knowing Addi's lips had been where mine were.

We were quiet, enjoying the stillness around us. Filtered light came in the French doors, gray and dense.

"Foggy today." I noticed.

"A storm is coming. The weather report said it was going to be a bad one."

"I hope everyone is able to make it home in time for the day before it does."

She lifted her head again, and I was surprised to see tears in her eyes. Worried, I cupped her cheek. "Addi, baby, what's wrong?"

She covered my hand with hers. "Nothing. I'm just so happy. I'm here. With you. Our family is all around us. We're all safe." She sniffled. "You married me."

I had to smile as I bent and kissed her. It was rare she showed such a sensitive, vulnerable side of herself. Very few people ever saw it, but I knew the tender heart her outside shell hid. It was one of the many things I adored about her.

"We'll think good thoughts for everyone so they get home with their loved ones too."

"Okay," she replied, laying her head on my shoulder. Tenderly, I wiped away the wetness under her eyes. "No more crying, little elf. It's Christmas."

She reached up and tugged the jaunty pom-pom on my hat. "I like this."

"I found it on my chest. I assumed you wanted me to wear it." I tweaked her nose. "I confess I'm disappointed not to see you in your elf pajamas, Addi. I thought we'd both be festive this morning."

"Oh." She slipped out from between my legs and took a few steps back toward the fire. "You don't like my robe?"

It was a deep shade of forest green, long and thick, no doubt keeping her warm. "It's pretty."

"I have slippers."

I began to laugh as I noticed them for the first time. They were bright red, with bells on the curved toes. She wiggled her foot so the bell tinkled.

"Very cute."

"I got new pajamas," she murmured as she undid the belt of her robe and shrugged her shoulders. "What do you think?"

I swallowed at the sight of her in a red camisole, delicate and frothy, tied with a bow and trimmed in white fluffy stuff. It ended at her hips. The tiniest scrap of lace nestled between her legs. She held herself straight, her breasts high, the hard nipples visible through the thin material. Her hair hung past her shoulders in golden waves, and her eyes were sparkling with mischievousness. The firelight danced behind her, casting shadows and glimmers on her skin.

My cock hardened at the erotic tableau in front of me.

Rising up on my knees, I crooked my finger. "I think you need to come closer."

When she was in front of me, I slid my hands up her legs, pressing my face into her soft skin. I wrapped my fingers around the thin straps at her hips. "I think you're going to need a new set once I'm finished with you."

Then I tore the lace away from her body and took her to the floor. She wrapped her legs around my waist, the sound of the tinkling bells loud in the room. She grinned up at me. "You know they say every time a bell rings, an angel gets their wings."

I rocked against her. "Well, I have something for you, baby, but it ain't no wings. It's gonna make you fly, though." I slid through her heat, hitting her clit.

She whimpered.

"Santa's got a big package—just for you."

"Let's go then, Santa," she moaned. "I want my present."

I tugged open the bow between her breasts with my teeth, groaning at the sight of her nipples. "Trust me, little elf, I want to give it to you." I wrapped my lips around a plump nipple and sucked.

"Oh," she whispered. "Merry Christmas to me."

I grinned against her skin. I planned on making it very merry.

At least twice.

With the bad weather approaching, I insisted on driving the ATV we owned. We had gifts to take, making going by foot awkward, and if the storm was as bad as they were predicting, walking home might prove to be treacherous—even with a short distance. As we pulled up to the Hub, I noted many others had thought the same way we had. There were a few vehicles parked there, as well as Aiden's 4x4. With its heavy tires and chains, he would make sure everyone got home safely.

We smiled in delight as we took in the building. Lights were strung around the windows, framing the wreaths hanging in each one. There was a tree outside decorated with red bows and suet balls for the birds. Santa and his reindeer were set up on the big deck—something I recalled from when I was a small child.

When we got inside, Addi gasped. Our family had been busy and decorated the entire place the last two days we'd been locked inside our home and lost in each other. Garland was strung, glowing with lights. Candles were plentiful, the scent of pine, holly berry, and cinnamon heavy in the air. Everywhere you looked, there was something Christmassy. The railings were wrapped in greenery and more lights, the mantel on the fireplace piled high with evergreens and pinecones. Bows adorned picture frames. Vases were filled with more pinecones and red balls. It was beautiful every year, and every time it felt as if we'd never seen it before. Something new had always been added, and it was fun to see familiar things as well as the unique additions.

The gift-laden tree was ablaze with color, the ornaments reflecting off the thousands of twinkle lights on the branches and the bows on the presents underneath. Every year, Bentley, Aiden, and my dad went out and chopped down a tree tall enough to fill the enormous space. The ceiling soared to twenty feet in the center, and the lowest point was still over twelve feet tall. Every year, they argued and measured and always brought home a tree Aiden was certain would fit. Every year, some had to be cut off the bottom and the branches trimmed. Every year, they quarreled like schoolboys. It was odd as a child, but as an adult, it was amusing. I realized it was simply their thing. One year, Van went with them and brought home a perfect-fitting tree. He gloated over the magnificence. The other three men sulked for days. He never went with them again.

The air was filled with delicious aromas. Turkey, ham, spices. The sweet fragrance of pies mixed with the scents of the candles. Christmas music was playing, and I heard the sounds of our family laughing and talking. I added our gifts to the pile, and we headed toward the kitchen and were greeted by our mothers and aunts. Hugs and kisses were plentiful.

Nan stood back, cupped my face, then Addi's, and kissed us. "No need to ask how you are." She winked. "You both look very happy."

"I'm sure Aiden will still ask," Cami chuckled. "Rudely, of course."

"And Bentley will smack him," Emmy added.

"So will Maddox," Mom smirked.

And they were right.

Bentley shook my hand, my dad enveloped me in a hug, and Aiden smacked my back. "How's married life?"

"Aiden," Bentley warned. "That's my daughter."

"And my son," Maddox added.

Aiden held up his hands. "Just asking." He grinned my way. "She calling *you* daddy now?"

I tried to hold in my laughter, but I couldn't. The remark was so Aiden. My dad tried to hide his smile and failed. Van and Halton both smirked, and Bentley choked on the cup of coffee he was drinking.

Luckily, the rest of the crew came up from downstairs and interrupted the moment. There was more laughter and teasing, although most of it didn't reach Bentley's ears. I knew Addi was getting some teasing as well from the flush across her cheekbones, but it was all in good fun.

Drink in hand, I followed the crew into the games room and admired the new air hockey table "Santa" had brought. Along with the foosball and pool tables already in place, it was a great addition.

"I wanted to add an ax-throwing area, but I was voted down," Aiden pouted.

"A little dangerous inside," Pops pointed out. "Fun, but dangerous."

Van perched on the edge of the pool table. "You know, the small area by the woodpile would be a great place. We could build an enclosure there. Safe. All cement walls lined in wood. A wood burner to keep it warm in the winter."

Aiden brightened. "Love it."

"Great sport," Bentley mused. "It could be fun. As long as it's not inside here."

"I'll draw up some plans."

Aiden high-fived him. "Awesome. I'll take on the boys."

"And we'll beat you," they said in unison.

"Whatever."

I headed toward Addi. I hadn't touched her in fifteen minutes—far too long. She was talking to Gracie, who smiled as I approached.

"Missing your bride?" she asked as I kissed Addi, then leaned over and brushed a kiss to her cheek.

"Yep." I looked around, lowering my voice. "Where's your, ah, *boss*?"

"You told him?" Gracie hissed in a low voice.

"Of course I did. It's Brayden."

"I'm not going to say anything. I won't give away your secret, Gracie." I shook my head. "But you really don't think it's going to come out?"

"No, it isn't," she snarled. "I'm not going to say anything, and neither are you."

"What about Jaxson?" I had a feeling he wasn't as anxious to hide this marriage as Gracie was.

"He isn't here and he's not coming, so there isn't going to be a problem. We'll get a fast, quiet divorce, and that will be the end of it."

"Wouldn't an annulment be faster?" Addi asked.

Gracie's face flushed, and I met Addi's startled gaze.

"Gracie," she whispered. "You didn't tell me that!"

"It doesn't matter. It happened. It's water under the bridge, and I'll deal with it."

"Does Jaxson have a say?" I asked.

"No. He knows it was a mistake. He's fine with it."

"Are you sure about that?" I asked, glancing over her shoulder out the window.

"Yes. No one will even remember meeting him in a couple of weeks."

"And you're sure he's not coming?" I asked again.

She glared at me. "First off, I uninvited him. And second, there's a huge storm coming, Brayden. Only an idiot would head out to Port Albany with the weather about to change."

I leaned close. "Then I guess your husband doesn't listen so well. And apparently, he *is* an idiot."

"What are you talking about?" she asked.

"Hey, look!" Ronan yelled at the same time. "Santa is outside!" Heads turned, and a ripple of laughter followed.

Gracie spun around and gasped.

Outside, Jaxson was on his way to the front door.

He was dressed as Santa, minus the beard, his dark hair unmistakable. He carried a large sack of what I assumed were gifts over his shoulder.

Addi looked at Gracie. "What is he doing?"

"He's playing Santa," she hissed.

"Why would he do that?" Addi queried, sharing a confused glance with me.

Gracie covered her face with her hands, her voice muffled. "Because apparently I talk too much when I'm drunk."

Addi began to laugh, covering her mouth with her hand to stifle it. "Oh dear."

I had to bite back my smile.

By now, Jaxson was almost at the door. Aiden was heading toward it, looking far too excited for a man his age.

Gracie grabbed my arm, her eyes wild with panic. "You need to stop him, Brayden!"

"Too late, I'm afraid." I murmured. "Even Aiden's into it."

"Oh god," she mumbled.

I couldn't help my smirk. "Good luck with that secret, Gracie. And by the way? We're *all* gonna remember this."

I was pretty sure she told me to go fuck myself as she brushed past me.

I had to be mistaken, though. Gracie didn't swear. But the Gracie I knew wouldn't have gotten drunk and married in Vegas either.

I guessed I had heard right.

Huh.

CHAPTER 7
ADDISON

I moved closer to Brayden, watching as Gracie hurried toward the door, determined to beat Aiden there. Her short legs had no chance of catching up to his long strides, especially when he was hurrying. He beat her, throwing open the door.

Jaxson filled the frame. He looked ridiculous and yet totally perfect. He wore a heavy red Santa jacket, complete with a belt cinched over an obviously padded stomach. His hat was perched on his head, slightly askew, the white pom-pom bouncing in the wind. The red was vivid against his almost black hair. His chiseled jaw bore a trace of scruff on it, highlighting the rugged handsomeness of his face.

Brayden leaned down. "Stop staring, little elf. Or I'll get jealous."

I rolled my eyes. "I'm married, not dead. Santa didn't look like that when we were kids."

He chuckled.

Aiden greeted him, his booming voice filling the room. "Santa! Come on in!"

Jaxson stepped in, lowering his bag to the floor. His gaze found Gracie quickly, and I saw the way his eyes lit up when he saw her. She was glaring at him, her hands tightened into fists at her sides. He winked at her, not at all perturbed by her lack of warmth or greeting.

He cleared his throat and put his hands on his hips. "Ho ho ho."

I tried not to laugh but failed. He wasn't exactly jolly. He tried again, lifting his arms. "Merry Christmas!"

He looked shocked at the chorus of Merry Christmases he got in return. But he smiled, and the gesture transformed his face from handsome to sinfully sexy.

"What's in the bag, Santa?" Ronan yelled.

"I hope it's booze!" Thomas added.

Jaxson blinked and looked at the bag by his feet. "Some of it," he said, sounding doubtful.

Aiden laughed and clapped him on the shoulder. "Some is good. Let's get this party started."

I sat beside Gracie, watching as Jaxson slowly walked around the room. I was fascinated observing him. He spoke to every person, called them by name, reached into his bag and handed them a present. They were simple things, but thoughtful. Chocolates or bath bombs for all the girls, cigars or small totes of alcohol for the men, each one tailored to the individual's taste. Every single one had a festive ribbon attached.

"He must have spent hours buying everything," I mused. "Never mind getting a suit and braving the weather to come here."

Gracie made a low noise in her throat. I glanced at her. She was focused on him intently, her hands clenched into fists on her lap.

"How on earth did he remember everyone's name?" I wondered out loud. "He hasn't made a single mistake."

"He does that," she murmured. "He remembers faces and names. Facts. The smallest details others forget."

"Amazing."

"It makes him a good lawyer," she admitted.

I grabbed her hand and squeezed it. "It makes him a good person too. He's extremely generous. And thoughtful."

"I told him not to come," she muttered almost to herself. "Why did he come?"

"Apparently, he wanted to," Brayden interjected cheekily. "Maybe it was his Christmas wish."

"Shut it," Gracie snarled.

Brayden smirked, clearly enjoying himself. I had to admit it was amusing to see Gracie acting so un-

Gracie-like. Normally unflappable and still, she was a bundle of nerves. Her color was heightened, and her foot swung in agitation. Her little huffs of annoyance were adorable.

She tensed further as he approached the parents. He'd handed out something to all the "juniors," as Aiden called our generation, except for the three of us. I had a feeling he was saving that for last.

He shook all the dads' hands and kissed the mothers on the cheek. He thanked them profusely for including him today and handed them each a present. They were gracious and warm in return. Gracie was so anxious when he stood in front of Richard, I was sure she had stopped breathing. She almost growled when her dad clapped him on the shoulder, thanking him for the scotch. Her mom, Katy, spoke to him at length, listening to his low-voiced replies. At one point, her hand lifted to rest on his bicep as if in comfort.

"What is he *doing*?" Gracie whispered. "Why is he still up there? Why is he acting so…*nice*?"

"Is he not usually nice?" I asked.

"He's known as 'the dick' around the office," she replied. "He yells a lot."

"Just like your dad in his younger years—on both counts." Brayden rubbed his hands together in glee. "Oh, the apple doesn't fall far from the tree, does it, Gracie?"

"You want to wear that coffee, Bray? Keep it

up," Gracie snarled. "*Why* is he still talking to my parents?"

Brayden chuckled. "Chatting to his new in-laws. I think your dad likes him. Your mom does, for sure. He'll fit in nicely once they get over the shock."

"Shut it, asshole," she growled.

I lifted my eyebrows at her vehemence.

"Just answering your question." Brayden defended himself. He grinned widely. "Maybe you should join him. Get them used to you as a couple."

"I'm going to slash your tires, and you'll have to walk home. I hope you freeze."

"What about my wife? Your best friend?" he asked, not at all concerned.

"She can stay with me."

"Hmm," he mused. "Three's a crowd. If the storm is bad, Jaxson is gonna have to stay over. I bet he chooses your bed to rest his weary bones." He winked lewdly at her. "His *rights* and all as your hubs."

She glared, her gaze colder than the wind blowing outside. "Get stuffed, Bray."

"I think that's his job."

"Stop it, both of you," I interrupted. As amusing as their banter was, I didn't want to miss a second of the action happening around me. Jaxson didn't strike me as only acting nice. He seemed intense but not mean or nasty. I wondered if perhaps people found his forceful nature off-putting. Maybe it was an act. People found me cold. Those who knew me best knew I was anything but. It was the persona I used to protect myself from the outside world. I peeked over at Gracie. Had she ever considered that? Had she really never seen this side of Jaxson?

Jaxson handed both Nan and Pops their gifts and received another kiss from Nan and a handshake from Pops. Again, he stood and spoke to them, seemingly at ease. Then he turned and headed our way.

Gracie pushed herself farther into the corner of the sofa.

He sat across from us, pulling off his hat and running his hand through his hair. He offered us a rueful smile. "This being Santa is tiring stuff. No wonder it only happens once a year."

Gracie shook her head. "There was no need for all the gifts, Jaxson. Or to risk your life to drive here. You should probably head back before the storm gets worse."

I gaped at her rudeness, but he only smiled. "Your mother and aunts were kind enough to invite me here today so I wouldn't be alone on Christmas. I still have the four-wheel drive, so I was perfectly fine on the roads, although I appreciate your concern. And to show up empty-handed would have been rude."

"A bottle of wine would have sufficed. This—" she waved her hand "—is a little overboard."

"There, I beg to differ. I recall being told that

Santa's visit made the entire day magical. How can one ignore a chance to do that?" He paused, his voice lowering as he stared at her. "Especially for you, Gracie."

I tried not to giggle.

She sniffed, turning her head as if she could ignore his presence. Brayden and I exchanged a glance. The sexual tension between them was palpable. His gaze locked on her no matter where he was in the room, and whether Gracie admitted it or not, hers did as well. His words said so much. Why wasn't Gracie listening?

With them sitting that close to each other, you could feel something between them. How on earth they thought no one would catch on today was laughable. I had a feeling today was simply a ticking time bomb, and I wondered who would be caught in the explosion.

Jaxson handed me a lovely box of chocolates and Brayden a small bottle of his favorite whiskey. As with his dad, it was his preferred alcohol, although he didn't enjoy sampling as much as Maddox did. Brayden had a brand, and he stuck to it.

Ignoring the look Gracie threw me, I stood and kissed Jaxson's cheek. "Thank you. How on earth did you know these are my favorites?"

He smiled. "I listen." He glanced at Gracie. "I'm always listening." He reached into the bag and withdrew a box of chocolate caramels—Gracie's favorite. The box was larger than the others had been and decorated beautifully. "For my favorite intern."

"I'm your only intern."

"Yes, you are. You are both."

She took the box, touching the lovely bow. I noticed the way her fingers trembled. "Thank you."

Jaxson folded the bag beside him. "I guess my work is done." He stood and pulled off his heavy Santa coat and removed the padded stomach. His actions revealed a white dress shirt, covered in a deep navy cable-knit cardigan. He looked casual but dressy at the same time. I noticed the way Gracie's gaze flickered up and down, then she looked away. He was incredibly well built and sexy. A cross between Aiden and Brayden. Tall and strong. Broad yet slim. I could only imagine the muscles his clothes hid. I had to avert my eyes.

He reached into a pocket of his coat beside him and handed me an envelope. I frowned.

"What is this?"

"For you and your husband."

Confused, I opened it, finding a wedding card with a donation receipt to the local no-kill shelter we supported. It was generous and kind. Thoughtful.

"You didn't have to do this."

He shook his head. "I enjoyed being at your wedding. Meeting your family. Being welcomed so warmly—" his gaze drifted to Gracie, then back to me "—by your family. I wanted to contribute to a cause so dear to your heart."

It was a thoughtful gesture. I met his gaze, seeing the flare of pain in his eyes as he spoke. He was intense and deep. Serious. But I had a feeling underneath was a man with many complex layers. And whether or not Gracie wanted to admit it, he was trying to open himself up to show her.

I stood and hugged him. "Thank you. I'm glad you're here today, Jaxson."

I ignored Gracie's muffled gasp of outrage. Brayden stood and shook his hand. "Up to a game of air hockey?"

"Sounds like fun."

"I'm going to help with dinner preparations. You coming with me, Gracie?" I asked.

She pursed her lips. "I would like a moment with Jaxson first."

Brayden grabbed my hand. "Okay. See you downstairs shortly."

I tried not to grin as I heard Jaxson's mutter. "If I survive."

BRAYDEN

Christmas was always fun. I knew this Christmas would be even more so, having just gotten married.

Add in the unexpected behavior and the secret Gracie was hiding?

It was awesome.

When Jaxson joined us, he was cool and calm. He admitted he had never played air hockey but caught on quickly. It was a top-of-the-line machine, complete with all the bells and whistles. Sounds that echoed when you scored. Buzzers. Crowd noises. The kids inside us loved it.

Jaxson was competitive and smart—a great opponent—and the room was loud with smack talk and laughter. I didn't push or try to get information. I liked to tease Gracie, but I wasn't an asshole. It was her secret to share, and I wouldn't break her confidence. It wasn't hard to notice the way he kept looking for her, though. Every time someone would walk into the room, his gaze would snap to the door. When the sound of a feminine voice would come closer, he would lift his head, and I knew he was hoping it was Gracie. He seemed genuinely infatuated with her, and I was dying to hear the story. His version. I had a feeling it was way different from hers.

We played, taking turns until Addi appeared downstairs. Her face was flushed, and she was wiping her hands on a dish towel. "Snacks are ready, and Aiden wants to get to the presents."

Everyone laughed. Aiden was always big on the presents. Funnily enough, his favorite part was watching people open the gifts and seeing their enjoyment. The big man was really just a giant teddy bear.

For the first time since arriving, Jaxson looked uncomfortable. He set down his pusher as the room emptied, the offer of food and gifts too tempting to resist.

"I believe I'll find a quiet corner and perhaps read for a while."

Addi shook her head, walking over and wrapping her arm through his. "No, you have to come join us."

"This is for family. Your gift time. I'm quite fine on my own."

She leaned close, smiling at him. "It's Christmas, Jaxson. Santa visits everyone here." She tugged on his arm. "*Everyone.*"

A delighted smile tugged on his mouth. "I don't wish to intrude. It wasn't my intention."

"You aren't intruding. And you have to come."

Watching how he responded to Addi, the way his tension melted under her gentle urgings, I understood. She was hard to resist. They walked past me, Addi holding on to his arm, making sure he wasn't left alone.

I followed behind, smiling.

And I fell in love with her all over again.

There were platters of sandwiches, bowls of chips and snacks, and trays of cookies. The spicy scent of hot cider laced the air. We all helped ourselves and headed toward the tree. Outside, the sky was heavy and the snow falling thick and fast.

"Thank god we're all here and safe," Nan breathed. "No one is leaving this compound until it's over."

We all laughed since none of us planned on doing so. Jaxson looked pleased at the thought, and I noticed the glance he and Gracie shared.

We ate, enjoying the food and one another's company. It was the same way all the time when we were all together. We seemed to drift into our own little pods. The triplets sat close together as usual, their dark heads bent over their plates. Liam sat next to them, and beside him, Aiden. All were quiet as they consumed their lunch. In the Callaghan family, eating was serious business. Cami and Ava were the softness in the family, yet I wouldn't want to cross either of them. Both were fierce and strong —in many ways, stronger than the boys. They were adored by all the males in the family.

Shelby was perched on the stairs, eating as she drew. She always had a sketchbook close at hand, and I knew she would be busy all day. My mom and dad were together on a sofa close to her, my mom making sure my sister ate since she tended to get lost in her art. My mom fussed over them, chiding my dad about how many stuffed pepper poppers he took and teasing him about heartburn. He responded by kissing her nose and telling her he was fine.

Bentley sat in a chair, Emmy perched on his lap. They always stayed close. He would often tuck a blanket over her knees and tug her shawl over her shoulder if it slipped off. She fed him tidbits, their intimate gestures never changing over the years. Thomas sat in a chair close to Bentley, the two of them talking quietly as they ate. I heard him telling his parents about some changes to the marine biology program and being excited by the new direction. They listened intently, obviously pleased to have their son close for a short time. Chloe sat nearby, her knees tucked to her chest, nibbling away, lost in thought.

Richard and Katy were nestled in the corner, Gracie perched close by and the twins, Gavin and Penny, talking up a storm as usual, often finishing each other's sentences. Their youngest, Matthew, was the quiet one of the group. He sat on the ottoman, listening and observing as always. Addi and I were beside them, and Jaxson had eased his big body to the floor, angled so he faced Gracie directly. She had relaxed somewhat and was cordial, although I had a feeling it was more to show her parents that all was well rather than how she really felt.

Not far away, Reed sat on the floor in front of Heather, his head leaning against her lap. They always sat between their two families, equal and happy.

Van and his girls sat together, Liv watching Reed with a smile. They loved Heather, and I knew they were hoping Reed made it official soon.

Reid and Becca and their crew were close to the tree. That was their spot and always had been. Reid was a big kid himself and loved the holidays. Halton and his gang rounded out our group. They took up a whole section of the room, and the laughter was constant with them.

Nan and Pops never sat anywhere for long. They perched and visited each group, checking everyone was good and that we were all happy. I knew Nan was disappointed that her grandson Colin and his family weren't here this year. It was his wife's turn to have Christmas with her family, but they would be here before New Year's. Jordan's kids stayed home this year since his eldest granddaughter was pregnant and too far along to travel. He and Nan were headed to BC in a few days and would have their holiday time with them then.

It occurred to me that one day, hopefully not too far in the future, Addi and I would have our own little pod. That our parents would be fussing over our child, and we would claim our own space in the room. The thought did something to my chest, warming it and making me smile.

Addi leaned close, whispering. "What are you

thinking about, Brayden? You're smiling like you just won the lottery."

I bent low and kissed her. I could do that now without worry. She was my wife, and Bentley could no longer clear his throat if he thought I was getting too close or lingering on her lips too long. I could kiss her anytime I wanted to. But I kept it respectful. For today.

"I did win the lottery. I got you." I kissed her again, making her smile. "I was thinking about the future, Addi. Adding our kids to this crazy mix. Watching them grow up the way we did, surrounded by this outrageous family."

Her eyes widened. "Can you imagine?" she whispered back.

"Yeah, I can. It's gonna be awesome."

"But we're going to wait a while."

I brushed my mouth to hers again. "Yes. I need you to myself for a while. Just you and me." I touched her cheek, drifting my fingers down her skin. "I'm not ready to share just yet." I moved in for another kiss when the familiar sound of a throat clearing caught my attention. I looked up and met Bentley's eyes. He waved his fingers between us, indicating he was still watching me, but he did so with a wink and a grin. I couldn't resist kissing Addi one last time.

He and I both chuckled.

After eating, we turned to the tree and the mountain of gifts it contained. Our tradition was that each person got a gift to open, and we all admired them. Nothing was hurried or rushed. When we were kids, it was different, but over the years, we had learned how to enjoy it. Savor the time. Admire the wrapping and the gift that lay under the festive bows.

Jaxson looked startled when he was handed his first gift. It was a handsome scarf, one I had, in fact, been admiring, and from the fast, apologetic look my mother cast me, I knew it was, indeed, the same one. But I was fine with it, especially seeing his delight. There was a nice bottle of scotch from Nan and Pops, and a few other gifts that he opened. Each one, he exclaimed over—even the socks we all got every year—and with each gift, I saw him relax and enjoy himself. I always knew the women in my family were special, but seeing how they had strived to make sure this man was included made me proud to be part of this family.

There were the usual gag gifts. Silk underwear for Aiden he was all too happy to model. A book, *101 Ways to Relax,* for Bentley. A pocket calculator for my dad. A tiny hammer for Van. Small things that made everyone laugh.

Addi got the raciest set of lingerie I had ever seen. Her cheeks were bright red as she held up the scraps of black lace, and I felt my ears get warm as I pictured her in it. The catcalls and whoops made me chuckle. The way the triplets high-fived one another left me no doubt who the culprits were.

The Costco-sized box of condoms I got made me laugh out loud.

After the gifts were done, we cleaned up the paper and lunch remnants. Some people drifted back to the basement. The women checked on dinner and then decided quiet relaxation with some wine was called for in the library. The snow had stopped, at least for now, so some donned their skates and headed outside.

I wanted a little time alone with Addi. We bundled up and went for a walk down by the water. The beach was covered in snow, piles beginning to accumulate by the rocks. The inner bay was frozen, and the laughter from the skaters floated over the air. We walked into the woods, finding a quiet spot. I pulled her into my arms and kissed her. She wrapped her hands around my neck, returning my caresses with enthusiasm. Moments passed as we lost ourselves to the other. The cold ceased to exist, the raging fire of desire racing through me. I gathered her close and pulled her to my lap as I sat down heavily on a broken tree behind a clump of bushes. We were hidden and private. We kissed, our tongues stroking together, at times deeply, other times teasing and light. I nibbled on her bottom lip, and she licked along my teeth and teased the roof of my mouth. I slid my fingers over her neck, holding her close. She whimpered as I thrust against the heat of her, wrapping her legs tight around my waist.

I broke away, burying my face into her neck. "If we don't stop, I am taking you right here," I warned.

"What's stopping you?"

"Explaining to your father how you got frostbite on your ass."

She began to giggle. Light, airy sounds that made me chuckle. I pulled her closer, letting her nestle into my chest. "Ah, Addi. I love you."

"I love you."

We sat in the silence, wrapped around each other.

The sounds of footsteps approaching startled us, and we looked at each other. Addi raised her finger to her lips, telling me to stay silent. Hopefully whoever it was wouldn't notice us sitting off the path and keep moving. I knew Aiden was planning on a marshmallow roast, and it was probably him looking for branches to whittle for it later.

But it wasn't Aiden.

"Okay, Jaxson, we've gone far enough. You wanted privacy, you got it. Now say whatever it is you want to say."

Addi's panicked gaze met mine, and I shrugged.

"Is it wrong for a man to want a few moments alone with his wife on Christmas Day?"

"I'm not your wife."

"I have a certificate that says otherwise."

"Stop it, Jaxson. It was a mistake."

"I disagree."

She huffed a sigh, the sound so Gracie-like, I had to bite back my laughter.

There was movement, and Gracie spoke.

"What is that?" she said, sounding horrified.

"A Christmas gift for you."

"I don't want a gift."

"Too bad, my darling. Take it."

There was a beat of silence, and he spoke again. "Take it now, or I'll hand it to you in front of your family."

The sound of paper being torn met my ears, and I shared an amused glance with Addi. Jaxson was a determined man.

"*What* have you done? This is not necessary, Jaxson."

"Our rings didn't fit. I wanted you to have a real one. One as beautiful as you."

"I am not your wife!"

"Yes, you are."

"We both know I married you drunk and out of my mind. We're getting a divorce."

His reply cut through the air, the lone word potent. "No."

"Give me one good reason why not."

There was the sound of rustling and a muffled gasp, followed by silence, then a low, almost painful sound.

Curious, Addi and I leaned over, tugging aside the branches that concealed us.

Gracie was locked in Jaxson's arms, and he was kissing her. The interesting part, considering how much she protested, was that she was kissing him back. He had her hair fisted in his hands, holding her tight to his mouth. She gripped his neck, her fingers moving restlessly on his skin. The low moans they both made were erotic.

I sat back, letting the branches fall into place. I gazed at Addi, her eyes wide with shock. I knew she wanted to stand up—let them know we were here, but it was too late. We had to hope they moved on.

I only prayed they didn't get carried away and stumble in our direction, looking for a place to continue their amorous clutch.

That was going to be awkward.

Suddenly, there was movement, and Gracie gasped. "Stop doing that!"

"Why? Give in, Gracie. Admit you feel something, and let's work on it. Tell your family. I'll stand by you."

"I am not staying married to you."

"Yes, you are."

Something shiny and bright sailed over our heads. It landed beside Addi, and she picked it up, staring at it. A thick band set with diamonds glittering in the overcast, muted light. It was beautiful and elegant. Much like Gracie.

When she wasn't furious and spitting like a

crazy person. I wasn't sure I could get used to this side of her.

"That's what I think of your gift and this marriage. It's not happening, Jaxson. Keep your gifts and your lips to yourself!"

"Gracie," he admonished gently.

"I mean it, Jaxson. I will be polite because my mother and aunts invited you. You leave as soon as dinner is over, and I don't want to see you until I return to the office. And the first thing we're going to do is file for divorce."

She stomped away. I waited for an outburst from Jaxson. Expletives. But he was silent. Then he spoke up.

"Please tell me you found the ring."

We shared a startled glance, and he appeared around the bushes we were behind. Addi held up the ring. "We did."

"You knew we were here?" I asked.

He shrugged. "If Grace hadn't been so irritated, she would have noticed the footprints as well. She was determined not to go farther, so I just let her speak."

"She's not usually so…" Addi trailed off.

"Angry? Hurtful?"

"Yes."

He held out his hand, and she dropped the ring into his palm. He studied it for a moment, then slid it into his pocket.

"I hurt her first. I need to make it up to her."

He paused. "I was correct then when I had assumed she confided in you, Addi? She told me how close you are."

"She did," Addi confirmed, her voice low. "She's determined to end this marriage. She insists it was a mistake."

He frowned, looking sad and forlorn for a moment. Then he shook his head. "It was not. And I am as determined to keep her as she is determined to be rid of me."

"Why?" I asked before I could stop myself.

He looked at me as if I were crazy.

"Because she is the only warmth in my life. Without her, the cold will destroy me."

His words hung heavy in the air. I had no idea how to reply to a statement that profound.

He cocked his head to the side, studying us. "Thank you for keeping our secret. One day, you will no longer have that burden."

He turned and left, his footsteps heavy and measured.

Addi looked at me. "What the hell was that?"

His footsteps faded, and I whistled. "I hope Gracie is prepared. That was a man determined to win." I looked down at her. "And I don't think he'll fight fairly."

"Oh boy."

ADDISON

Taking advantage of the break in the storm, Brayden and I walked a bit more, watched the skaters, and even had a snowball fight. We sat by the fire Aiden had started, warming up and enjoying the quiet. Brayden whittled some sticks for marshmallows later. Aiden joined us, and between them, they got a large pile done. Aiden was quiet at first, his knife moving over the ends fast.

"Great wedding," he suddenly said.

Brayden snickered. "Yeah, it was."

"You're not mad at me, are you? I really wanted to give the toast."

I flung myself into his massive arms, hugging him tight. "We would have been disappointed if you hadn't," I assured him. "You were very funny."

"Bentley smacked me later and refused to give me a cigar. Mad Dog snuck me one, though, so I figured if he was okay with it, you would be."

"We were more than okay."

He relaxed and started telling us some funny stories, sounding more like Aiden. It hadn't even occurred to me he'd be worried. It was strange how weddings and holidays seemed to make people more emotional. I was glad he said something so we could reassure him. He hugged me again before we left to head inside, holding me tight.

"Love you, Addi-girl," he whispered, using his old nickname for me.

"Love you back, Uncle A."

He stood with a grin. "I'm still your favorite, right?"

"Always."

We left him smiling and happy.

I was beginning to feel tired, and I wondered how early we could head home. Between the wedding and Christmas and all the hidden drama, I felt drained.

Brayden kissed my head. "I'll whisk you away after supper. We can have a bath and some sleep, okay, little elf?"

"You know me too well."

He stroked under my eye, his touch gentle. "I know this little bruise forming means you've had enough. No one will think twice about us cutting out a little early. Technically, we're on our honeymoon."

I was grateful for that excuse.

I wasn't sure what to expect when we got back to the Hub, but luckily, everything seemed fine. Jaxson was in the library reading, and Gracie was in the kitchen. Brayden kissed me, then went to find his dad, hoping for a game of chess. They started one each Christmas day, and it usually lasted until the New Year. They would take long breaks, sometimes a day between moves, trying to outdo each other. Maddox often won, although Brayden had beaten him two years in a row.

Gracie smiled as I walked into the kitchen.

Her cheeks were flushed and her eyes bright. I spied a bottle of wine on the counter—her favorite kind—and it was half empty. It was unusual for her to drink so much, but I supposed given the stress she was feeling, it was understandable. I poured myself a glass of red and asked what I could do to help.

My mom smiled at me. "You can make the gravy in a bit. The boys set the tables, the turkeys will be out soon, and dinner is in about an hour. Did you and Brayden have a nice walk in the woods?"

Gracie's gaze snapped to mine, and I smiled innocently. "We walked on the beach and watched them skate. We mostly sat by the fire and whittled sticks with Aiden."

I saw Gracie visibly relax.

"Why don't you take your wine and sit by the tree? You've been going all day. I'll call when it's gravy time."

I took her up on her offer and curled up by the tree. Shelby was busy sketching on the other end of the sofa. Ronan was asleep on another. Thomas was busy on his laptop, listening to someone in his earbuds, but he offered me a smile and a wink as I sat down.

Outside, the snow was getting heavier and harder. The wind was picking up as the sun went down, and I had a feeling Jaxson wouldn't be going anywhere. I thought about what he'd said about hurting Gracie. I wondered if she would ever tell me the whole story.

How had I missed the fact that something huge was happening in her life, and I didn't know about it? I had been so caught up in the opening of the winery, the wedding, and everything else, I had missed the signs. She had been quieter than normal, and we hadn't seen much of each other outside of work. I vowed to do better once the holidays were over.

She walked into the room just as Jaxson appeared across the way. They stood looking at each other. His pain was evident in his gaze. Her anger colored her vision, and she glared at him and turned on her heel and walked away.

He watched her leave with a slight shake of his head, and he headed downstairs, disappearing from view.

For the first time ever, I wanted Christmas done. We really needed to talk.

BRAYDEN

Dinner was its usual loud, boisterous affair. There was so much food. Platters of turkey and ham. My mom's garlic mashed potatoes plus a huge dish of roasted ones. Liv's curried cheese vegetables—the yams, carrots, and cauliflower tasty with a bite of curry and the rich sauce. Massive containers of stuffing. Platters of warm buns. Vast boats of gravy my wife had made.

Dishes of homemade cranberry sauce, festive in color. An area filled with nothing but cookies and tarts, pies, and sweets. A feast made with love by all the women in our lives, including my wife. I grinned, thinking about how much I loved calling Addi *my wife*.

Tables were set up like a U, and there was a lot of shouting and passing of platters. It always shocked me that no matter how much food was prepared, it disappeared. The Callaghan boys, their father included, were frightening when it came to meals. I noticed Jaxson was fascinated, watching them devour plate after plate of food. He informed the mothers he had never seen a feast such as this or tasted food so delicious. There was no doubt all the women found him charming, Addi included, except for the one he wanted to charm the most.

The food vanished, the wine flowed freely, lulling us all into a sated, quiet mood. The dishes were loaded into the two dishwashers, and everyone drifted to their favorite spot for some downtime. A lot of bodies were napping. Some reading. Some simply relaxing. Richard sat across from Gracie, scrolling through his phone, showing her amusing pictures at times. She had finally relaxed, the wine she had been sipping catching up to her. I felt relief at the fact that the day was almost over and Gracie's bombshell remained a secret. She could figure it out with Jaxson and move on. I knew she would tell her parents once it was done, although I was sure some of the details would be glossed over. She would make it sound like an amusing incident, and she would close this chapter.

I was an idiot to think so.

It happened so innocently. So quickly. Jaxson stood, announcing that he was going to leave. There was a chorus of objections he waved aside, insisting he would drive slowly and the vehicle he had rented had four-wheel drive and snow tires. He assured everyone he had only drunk one glass of wine and was fine. He stated he had work to do and had to return home. He kissed all the mothers and Nan, shook the hands of the dads and Pops, his gratitude sincere and honest.

He headed in our direction, obviously planning on saying goodnight to Richard and the rest of us. Gracie set aside her wineglass, watching him come closer with mounting anxiety. Richard glanced her way with a frown, as if noticing her reaction to Jaxson. He narrowed his eyes, suddenly watchful.

One moment, Jaxson was striding toward us, and the next moment, he stumbled over the edge of a throw rug. He righted himself quickly, but his cardigan caught on the edge of a table, pulling at his pocket. The ring he had slid inside earlier flew out, soaring through the air and hitting the floor with a metallic thud that seemed to echo. It rolled on the wood floor, landing in front of none other than Gracie. The heavy platinum band spun like a top, the diamonds catching the light, the last few circles reminding me of a lazy drunk wobbling side to side, before it stopped. Jaxson hurried forward, but Richard bent, picking up the ring and studying it.

"Pretty ring." He narrowed his eyes. "Why is it in your pocket?"

"I forgot it was there." Jaxson held out his hand. "If I may have it back, please."

Richard held out the ring, then pulled back, squinting as he read something inside the ring. Jaxson went pale, and I shut my eyes, knowing whatever was inside the ring had just brought the secret out.

"My Saving Grace?" Richard snarled. "Why does this say 'My Saving Grace'? Are you…" His eyes widened. "Are you having an *affair* with my daughter?" His voice rose. My dad jumped to his feet, heading in our direction, Aiden following. Addi and I stood, knowing what was about to happen would not be pleasant.

Richard's gaze swung to Gracie. "What is going on?"

"This is why I don't drink," Gracie said, then, once again, burst into tears.

"Are you screwing with my daughter?" Richard bellowed. "You're her *boss*!"

He stepped toward Jaxson, who shook his head. "No. Absolutely not."

Richard shook his hand, the diamonds catching the light. "Explain this!"

Jaxson sighed and dropped his hand. There was nowhere to hide anymore. "We're not having an affair, Richard. We're married."

For a moment, only the sound of Gracie's sobs filled the air.

From behind us, one of the Callaghan boys muttered, "Well, holy…*night.* I wasn't expecting that."

Then it happened. Richard's fist shot out so fast, none of us had time to react. I heard the sound of bone meeting bone, and Jaxson stumbled backward, the ring once again hitting the floor. It rolled under the sofa.

My dad sprinted over, wrapping his arms around Richard to hold him back. He was yelling and cursing, trying to get to Jaxson. Oddly enough, Gracie stood, blocking his way as Jaxson straightened up, holding his jaw. Katy stood mute and confused across the room, watching the scene unfold in front of her. My mom stood beside her, wrapping her arm around her shoulders in comfort as Katy covered her mouth.

"Talk about decking the halls," another voice spoke up.

"I told you this wouldn't stay secret," I stated to Addi.

Richard's wild gaze turned on me. "You knew?" he yelled. "You knew about this?" He struggled harder against my dad's grip. Dad looked startled then lifted his eyebrows, indicating the door, telling me silently to get out. Others began to file from the room. It was like the proverbial sinking ship. The rats were getting out.

Holy shit.

Another Christmas I was going to have to run for it. At least this time I had my shoes. I grabbed Addi's hand. "Time to go."

I tugged her unwillingly behind me. I heard my dad tell Jaxson to get out, and he followed close behind me. We headed to his rental, and I took the keys from his hands. He looked as if he was in shock, and I wasn't sure he should be driving.

I headed to our house in his SUV, the normally short drive seemingly taking forever. The windows were so covered in snow and ice, visibility was almost nonexistent, and I didn't stop to scrape them. I pulled up and turned off the engine, grateful to have arrived.

"I should just go," he muttered.

"You can't drive in this, Jaxson. It would be suicide."

We led him inside, and he sat down heavily on the sofa. Addi went and got the ice pack, pressing it to his rapidly swelling cheek.

"Gracie," he breathed. "I need to go back."

"No," I insisted. "You need to stay right here

and let Gracie figure this out with her family. You'll be involved soon enough."

"What just happened?" he asked in a daze.

I clapped him on the shoulder. "Welcome to the family, Jaxson. Brace yourself. It's gonna be a bumpy ride."

I sat down, pulling Addi to my lap. "Enjoying your honeymoon?" I quipped, trying to lighten the air. "What's a family holiday without a secret being leaked and fistfights happening? I mean, usually, it's the triplets and eggnog is involved, but at least this one was different."

"This is awful," she whispered.

"Christmas took an unexpected detour," I agreed. I hugged her close. "It's going to be okay, Addi. Somehow, it will be."

"What are we going to do?"

I looked over at Jaxson. I thought about Gracie's tears. Richard's fury. The chaos that had no doubt continued after we'd made our escape. I indicated Jaxson, sitting with his shoulders hunched over on our sofa. I kept my voice low.

"They need to figure it out, Addi. It's their story to tell. Their future to decide."

She rested her head on my shoulder. "Will we ever know what happened?"

I had to admit, I hoped so.

It was a tale I wanted to hear.

THE FATHER CIRCLE OF TRUTH

BENTLEY

I stared inside the large, elegant room, watching Addi move around, her dress floating like a cloud around her tiny frame. She looked so much like Emmy did when I married her. Young, beautiful—with her whole life ahead of her.

Where the hell did the time go?

It seemed like only yesterday I was holding her in my arms, cradling her safely. Protecting her from the world. I was the one to slay the monsters under her bed. I held her when she had a nightmare. Kissed away the tears when she scraped her knee. She always looked at me as if I were a hero who could do no wrong. As if I were the center of her universe.

And now, I had been replaced.

I took a long draw on the scotch in my glass, ignoring the cold that surrounded me.

I should have worn a coat.

I should have brought the bottle of scotch outside instead of just asking for a triple shot.

I should have pitched Brayden over the balcony when I had a chance.

I drained the glass, holding it against my chest.

Addi looked to Brayden now for comforting. It was his arms she sought for protection. His counsel she listened to. The little bastard had usurped me.

"Bent, you're growling."

I startled at the sight of Aiden and Maddox standing beside me. I hadn't even heard them come outside. Aiden handed me my coat.

"Emmy said you needed this."

I shrugged it on, not letting go of my glass.

Maddox chuckled and held up a bottle of scotch. "I thought maybe you needed this as well."

"You're going to have to share." Richard VanRyan appeared beside Maddox.

"I brought glasses," Reid offered.

Hal Smithers chuckled darkly. "I brought a second bottle."

Van's deep laughter echoed in the dark. "You guys are a sorry lot."

I glared at him. "Wait until Sammy's getting married. When some little shit steals your baby girl."

"Hey, that little shit is my son," Maddox protested.

I waved my hand. "I was talking in general terms."

He laughed. "You were talking in scotch-soaked terms. You know they were meant to be together, Bent."

He was right. Brayden was perfect for Addi. He respected her. Encouraged her. Let her fly. No one could be as proud of her as he was, aside from me. She was smart. Brilliant at running ABC. Another man might have felt diminished by her, but not Brayden. He was comfortable enough in his own skin to know how special she was. He knew the real Addi. The sweet, loving woman behind the stern mask she wore as a businesswoman. She was lucky to have him.

Maddox added some more scotch to my glass and filled up the other ones. We toasted in silence and sipped the liquor.

Jen appeared, a hand on his hip. "A BAM convention on the balcony. Six sorrowful-looking men, drowning themselves in scotch." He shook his head sadly, although his eyes danced with glee. "Six hot-looking men, I might add. I had hoped you would bypass the sob fest, but I came prepared." He walked over and lit the propane heater, the warmth almost instant. He indicated the cleaned-off table and the closed box on the surface. "You can sit and drink. I don't want any of you pitching over the edge into the water. And there are some cigars. At least be civil, sit, wallow, and have your smoke. Your wives will drag your sorry asses home when you're done."

"Our asses aren't sorry," Aiden chuckled. "We're here to support Bent."

Jen pursed his lips, ignoring Aiden. "And soon you'll all be crying about whose turn it is next. Wailing about the lost years." He sighed. "I've seen it before." He focused his gaze on me.

"Brayden and Addi are perfect for each other. You should be thrilled your daughter fell in love with such an upstanding young man. Have your little sulk and be done with it." He grabbed the second bottle of scotch. "One is enough. My god, for such brilliant businessmen, you're all such idiots at times. We'd be pouring you all into the limos."

He left, and we all stared at his retreating back.

"That was uncalled-for. We can handle our liquor." Aiden frowned.

"Some of us better than others." Maddox smirked.

"Shut up all of you," I grumbled, leaning forward and snagging a cigar. "It's not your daughter who got married." I cut off the end and lit it, letting the smoke escape. I rarely indulged, but I decided today I deserved it. "And I *am* happy. Brayden is an amazing partner for Addi. I just don't have to like it. Not right this minute. Right this minute, I get my goddamn wallow. My baby girl is all grown up, and I feel old."

Maddox blew out a perfect smoke ring. "So do

I. Wasn't it just yesterday they were babies and Reid here still dressed like a homeless bum?"

Aiden chuckled. "Remember the day he sat in his office with no pants on because he needed to do laundry?"

Reid laughed. "That was a long time ago. Before Becca."

"Thank god for Sandy," we all said in unison.

"Remember Friday afternoon meetings?" I mused. "Us and the babies."

"I loved those," Maddox mused.

"The baby circle of truth," Reid sighed.

Richard laughed. "You guys *are* a sorry lot. We have awesome kids. They have to grow up—it's part of life."

"I'll remind you of that when Gracie drags some schmuck home to meet you."

He chuckled. "I didn't kill Reed."

Van laughed. "He said you tried."

Richard sniffed. "If I had really tried, I would have succeeded."

We all laughed, knowing he was full of it. Richard got along well with Reed and had been surprisingly relaxed over their relationship.

"I found it hard when Heather first moved here," Richard admitted. "I worried constantly. Was she safe? Lonely? Was she eating? Would she tell me if she wanted to come home? Knowing she had Reed and the way he cared for her was, and is, actually very comforting."

That made sense in an odd sort of way.

"Gracie will be different," I warned. "The first-born thing." I eyed Richard through a haze of smoke. "What's with her boss? He's pretty intense."

Hal snorted. "Pot meet kettle."

I flipped him the bird, ignoring the laughter from the rest of them.

Richard shrugged. "He helped her get here. Apparently with all the problems with weather and broken-down planes, they got as far as Calgary, and it looked like they were stuck. He rented a four-wheel-drive SUV and drove like a madman to get her to the wedding. I had a good conversation with him. He's a little uptight, but decent. He thinks Gracie is a brilliant intern and will be a great lawyer. I know she says he is hard to work for, but they must get along all right. She said he asked to come today. I think he wanted to see the winery."

"Is that all?" Reid asked dryly.

"What else could there be?" Richard asked. "He's her boss and mentor. He's older than her. I think he was just curious."

I met Maddox's gaze, and he lifted an eyebrow. I was sure I had noticed a few glances between the two of them that were not boss/intern-like. I was certain Richard was in denial, but I wasn't about to argue with him. I could be wrong—my head was a little mixed up today, and it seemed to be getting worse.

The table was silent for a moment, the music

from inside muted. I looked at the bottom of my glass, wondering who drank my scotch. The glass was full only a minute ago.

Wasn't it?

"She's leaving," I groaned, peering through the patio glass. "She isn't coming to say goodbye."

Everyone laughed. "Because she'll be five minutes away and you'll see her in two days, Bent," Aiden pointed out. "Two days."

"Still." I stood and headed to the doors. Someone yelled about a cigar, but I kept going until I found Addi.

I made sure she knew I was happy for her and I would see her in a couple of days. I didn't want her to think I was too busy checking that all her uncles were okay not to say goodbye. She would be upset, and I couldn't have my baby girl upset on her wedding day. I welcomed Brayden to the family. It was the least I could do. Emmy pulled me in for a kiss as I went by, and I was pretty certain she propositioned me, but for some reason, none of the conversations were sticking in my head. Words floated by, but they were hard to grasp.

I returned to the table and picked up my glass.

"She's gone," I said morosely.

Someone clapped me on the back, and I shut my eyes.

Suddenly, Emmy was in front of me, shaking my shoulder, her beautiful dark eyes staring into mine. "Come on, Rigid. It's time to go home."

I looked around, noticing the balcony was empty except for Aiden. He winked at me, sipping his scotch. Someone had drunk all of mine.

Bastard.

"Is the wedding done?"

She smiled. She was so beautiful. Even more beautiful than the girl I married. I loved her more now than ever.

Her smile became wider. "I know."

"Am I drunk?" I whispered.

"Ah, a little. You knocked them back pretty fast." She tugged on my hands. "You need to go home to bed and sleep. You'll feel better in the morning."

"Weren't you going to have your wicked way with me?"

She laughed, wrapping her arm around my waist. "That was your line, and maybe we'll save that until the morning."

"Oh." I glanced over my shoulder. "Is Aiden coming with us?"

He stood, laughing. "Right behind you, Bent. Always am."

I had to smile.

He was. My best friend and business partner was always there. So were Maddox and my whole extended family. And I had my Emmy.

I was a lucky man.

Emmy squeezed my waist. "Yes, you are."

"Aiden?"

"Yeah?"

"I survived my baby girl getting married."

"You did good, Bent."

The balcony tilted a little. I leaned into Emmy but spoke over my shoulder to Aiden.

"Gonna pass out now."

"I was expecting that."

"Okay. Thanks."

And I was gone.

Thank you so much for reading A MERRY VESTED WEDDING. If you are so inclined, reviews are always welcome by me at your eretailer.

I have spent many hours with these characters. Encouraged by readers like you, I wanted to see what stories the next generation would tell.

If you loved our unsuspecting new father-in-law Richard, the VanRyan's story begins with my series The Contract. You meet an arrogant hero in Richard, which makes his story much sweeter when he falls.

If happily ever afters are what you crave, I have a collection of short love stories for you to binge on in my Happily Ever After Collection.

Keep reading to find out what exactly happened before maid-of-honor, Gracie found her way to the wedding venue.

Enjoy reading! Melanie

SNEAK PEEK
MY SAVING GRACE

GRACE

I woke up, my head aching and my limbs feeling heavy. I blinked in the darkness of the room, my mouth feeling like the Sahara Desert. The room was unfamiliar, and it took me a moment to recall I was in a hotel room in Las Vegas.

Why did my head ache so badly?

I searched through my memories of the day before. Finally resolving the mystery of the trademark and copyright fiasco. Rushing to the airport, only to find out my plane was canceled due to an engine malfunction and the earliest flight I could get out was the next day. It was a long-ass flight with lots of stopovers, but it would at least get me home the night before Addi's wedding. I would miss the party but be there for the wedding. It was the best I could do. I returned to the hotel disappointed and upset. I hadn't wanted to come on this trip so close to her nuptials, but my jackass of a boss had insisted.

Jaxson Richards was a brilliant corporate lawyer. When I found out I would be interning with him, I was excited. His reputation preceded him. His track record spoke for itself.

The day I met him was forever etched into my memory. I had interviewed at the firm and was offered an intern position. On my first day, they explained I would intern with two lawyers over the course of my year in order to learn more during my time with them. I knew interns were often hired at the end of their stint, but I planned on working with the lawyer at BAM and cutting my teeth there before moving to ABC. Bill held a wealth of knowledge, and I wanted to soak it up before he retired and someone younger took his place.

I was sent to Jaxson's office, and I knocked on the door, waiting until he called out for me to enter. He sat behind his massive desk, and the moment our eyes met, my world tilted.

Tall and broad, stern and fierce, he stared at me, rising from his chair. His eyes were like iced fire, the blue vivid and clear. His hair was so dark it was almost black and brushed to gleaming. His suit fit him perfectly, and as he strode toward me, I caught a glimpse of his powerful thighs, large hands, and wide chest. He held out his hand, a smile tipping up one corner of his full lips and making the cleft in his chin prominent. I had never seen a man as handsome in my life. Considering the caliber of the group of men around me all the time, that was saying something.

"Grace VanRyan, I presume?"

I slipped my hand into his and shook it. The shock that tore through me at his touch startled me. For a moment, I was speechless, my throat dry, the words I needed to say unclear. I shook my head and found my voice, wondering why I was suddenly so nervous.

"Mr. Richards. Yes, I'm Grace." I cleared my throat, my words sounding strangely breathless. "It's a pleasure to meet you. I look forward to our time together."

He tilted his head. "As do I."

He escorted me to the chair across from him and waited until I sat down. It was only then I realized he was still holding my hand. He released his grip and sat down, resting his elbows on his desk. Then he asked me the strangest question.

"Tell me about Grace VanRyan."

I had expected him to ask about school. What I wanted to get out of the internship. My thoughts on the future. Not to ask about me.

"Nothing much to tell, really. I'm pretty boring."

"I find that hard to believe." He smiled, lifting one eyebrow. "You may be at the beginning of your story, Ms. VanRyan, but I doubt you're boring."

It slipped out before I could stop myself. "Gracie. My friends call me Gracie."

He inclined his head, that crooked smile once again gracing his lips. "Gracie," he repeated.

He sat back, not pushing the subject any further. He spoke of the firm, his history, and what he expected of me. We discussed some of the cases he was working on.

"Why corporate?" he asked.

"I've always been fascinated with it," I confessed. "My father is in marketing, so he always talked about trademarks and copyrights. I loved it when I went into the office with him, and I always snuck into the legal department and asked a thousand and one questions."

"VanRyan—VanRyan," he repeated. "Richard VanRyan?"

"Yes."

"I know his work."

I smiled, unsure what to say.

He went over the hours, where I would work, and answered all my questions. He smiled at me, the gesture turning his stern face into one of warmth, filled with personality.

"Your enthusiasm is to be commended. I look forward to having you under me."

My eyes widened, and he hastened to correct himself. "Work under me. With me. I have a feeling we'll make quite the team."

I had to push aside the thought of being under him. How his powerful body would feel against mine. The pleasure those large hands could bring. I felt my cheeks flush, and I had to lower my gaze before he noticed. There was silence, and then he cleared his throat and asked me a few more questions.

I shook my head to clear it, knowing I couldn't have such thoughts about the man who would be my boss, and responded in the proper manner, my mind fixed firmly on business.

Finally, he stood, buttoning his jacket, indicating our time was done.

After confirming my hours for tomorrow, I left, already excited about working with him. Learning.

I had no idea the greatest lesson I would learn would be heartache.

I tried to tamp down the painful memories.

How the excitement led to pain. How I discovered his charm hid a selfish man intent on only his own pleasure. Realizing to my horror I had fallen in love with someone incapable of returning that love and who had lied to me with his sweet words and gestures. The future I envisioned was nothing but a lie.

The face he showed the world was nothing but a lie.

I had no choice but to work with him every day, hiding my pain. Wondering how love could become hate. I refused to let him see my inner turmoil. To beat me. I was determined to finish this internship, walk away, and never see Jaxson Richards again. I hadn't wanted to come on this trip, but the partners, and Jaxson, had given me no choice.

I groaned as I shifted, the pain in my head changing from a dull ache to a constant pounding.

As I moved, I stiffened as I realized the weight on my hip wasn't that of the blanket, but of a hand.

My stomach rolled when reality hit me. Someone was in bed with me. I had slept with a stranger. I got drunk in Vegas and slept with a stranger. How clichéd.

Ignoring the ache in my head, I shot out of bed, yanking the blanket with me. I fumbled around, finding the light and switching it on. I squinted as the pain shot through my temple, and I gasped when I recognized the man lying in the bed beside me. Not looking upset at all, Jaxson pulled himself up into a sitting position and had the nerve to smile at me.

"Not a stranger," he said, letting me know I had spoken my thought out loud. "How are you feeling, darling?"

"What the hell are you doing here?"

"Until a few moments ago, I was sleeping. You must need some Tylenol. Let me get it for you."

"Don't bother. I meant how the hell did you get into my bed?"

He smirked, lifting one leg up to his chest and reclining back with his hands beneath his head. He looked too handsome and far too comfortable for this situation.

"Since this is my room, you're the one in *my* bed."

I looked around, seeing he was right.

"What the hell happened?"

"I would think that was obvious." He indicated the torn condom wrappers. "We had sex."

I gaped at him. "Why did I have sex with you? I don't like you!"

He leaned forward, his blue eyes bright in the dim light. His smile was wicked, and I wanted to wipe it off his face with my fist. "You *really* liked me last night. At least three times."

We'd had sex three times?

"At least," he confirmed. "I'm not counting the orgasm in the elevator, and I think I missed one other fuck. Against the wall, I think."

I was stunned. I stared at him, horrified. I had slept with my boss. Again.

"I can't believe I did that," I mumbled, gripping the blanket.

"That's not the only thing you did, darling."

"What could be worse?"

He tilted his head, studying me closely. He indicated my hand gripping the blanket.

"You married me."

A thin, too-tight band encircled my ring finger. He held up his hand, showing me a matching ring.

"How about that for cliché, Mrs. Richards?" He smirked.

The room spun, and my stomach heaved.

The last thing I remembered was his shout before the floor rushed toward me.

Unconsciousness had never been so welcome.

Preorder Book 1 of the new ABC Corp Series - My Saving Grace

ALSO BY MELANIE MORELAND

The Contract Series

The Contract (The Contract #1)

The Baby Clause (The Contract #2)

The Amendment (The Contract #3)

Vested Interest Series

BAM - The Beginning (Prequel)

Bentley (Vested Interest #1)

Aiden (Vested Interest #2)

Maddox (Vested Interest #3)

Reid (Vested Interest #4)

Van (Vested Interest #5)

Halton (Vested Interest #6)

Sandy (Vested Interest #7)

Vested Interest/ABC Crossover

A Merry Vested Wedding

ABC Corp Series

My Saving Grace

Insta-Spark Collection

It Started with a Kiss

Christmas Sugar

An Instant Connection

An Unexpected Gift

Mission Cove

The Summer of Us Book 1

Standalones

Into the Storm

Beneath the Scars

Over the Fence

My Image of You (Random House/Loveswept)

Happily Ever After Collection

Revved to the Maxx

Heart Strings

The Boss

ACKNOWLEDGMENTS

As always, I have some people to thank. The ones behind the words that encourage and support. The people who make my books possible for so many reasons.

Lisa—many thanks for being as awesome as you are.

Beth, Trina, Melissa, Peggy, and Deb—thank you for your feedback and support.
Your comments make the story better—always.

Kim—you are Karen's dream come true. LOL!

Karen—you wanted this—you asked for it repeatedly. I hope it makes you smile.
You make me smile every damn day.

To all the bloggers, readers, and especially my promo team. Thank you for everything you do. Shouting your love of books—of my work, posting, sharing—your recommendations keep my TBR list full, and the support you have shown me is deeply appreciated.

To my fellow authors who have shown me such kindness, thank you.
I will follow your example and pay it forward.

My reader group, Melanie's Minions—love you all.

Matthew—all my love—now and always.

ABOUT THE AUTHOR

NYT/WSJ/USAT international bestselling author Melanie Moreland, lives a happy and content life in a quiet area of Ontario with her beloved husband of thirty-plus years and their rescue cat, Amber. Nothing means more to her than her friends and family, and she cherishes every moment spent with them.

While seriously addicted to coffee, and highly challenged with all things computer-related and technical, she relishes baking, cooking, and trying new recipes for people to sample. She loves to throw dinner parties, and enjoys traveling, here and abroad, but finds coming home is always the best part of any trip.

Melanie loves stories, especially paired with a good wine, and enjoys skydiving (free falling over a fleck of dust) extreme snowboarding (falling down stairs) and piloting her own helicopter (tripping over her own feet.) She's learned happily ever afters, even bumpy ones, are all in how you tell the story.

Melanie is represented by Flavia Viotti at Bookcase Literary Agency. For any questions regarding subsidiary or translation rights please contact her at flavia@bookcaseagency.com

Connect with Melanie

Like reader groups? Lots of fun and giveaways! Check it out Melanie Moreland's Minions

Join my newsletter for up-to-date news, sales, book announcements and excerpts (no spam). Click here to sign up Melanie Moreland's newsletter

or visit https://bit.ly/MMorelandNewsletter

Visit my website www.melaniemoreland.com